I0611380

THE EDDAN COLLECTIVE

ALSO BY JOANNA DEMERS

Steal This Music:
How Intellectual Property Law
Affects Musical Creativity

Listening Through the Noise:
The Aesthetics of Experimental Electronic Music

Drone and Apocalypse:
An Exhibit Catalog for the End of the World

Anatomy of Thought Fiction:
CHS Report, April 2214

THE EDDAN COLLECTIVE

JOANNA DEMERS

Angelico Press

First published in the USA
by Angelico Press 2023
Copyright © Joanna Demers 2023

All rights reserved:
No part of this book may be reproduced or transmitted,
in any form or by any means, without permission

For information, address:
Angelico Press, Ltd.
169 Monitor St.
Brooklyn, NY 11222
www.angelicopress.com

paper 978-1-62138-944-6
cloth 978-1-62138-945-3

Book and cover design
by Michael Schrauzer

CONTENTS

INTRODUCTION

WE BEGIN THUS:

*My colleagues, in the enjoyment of the seemingly positive
changes brought about under the Eddan Collective, forgave
my naiveté. Posterity, which experienced the fatal effects of
my theories and speculations, will justly consider me as the
principal author of the decline of the American university.*

We of the Center for Humanistic Studies cite this
passage from the notes of Annika Trent, an American
historian writing in the twenty-first century. Trent, in
turn, took this passage from Edward Gibbon, an English
historian writing in eighteenth century. The book from
which Trent cribbed these sentences is a sprawling work
of over three thousand pages that tells of the decline
and fall of the Roman Empire. But we who attempt
to write a history of the dissolution of the American
university, and the erasure of the humanities from
academic curricula, do not know how to write history.
We could have told this story with a few sentences:

*In 2016, the first meeting of what would eventually be called
the Eddan Collective took place. The professional successes
of one of the Eddans' co-founders attracted substantial
funding for the group. Paradoxically, that institutional
support made it possible for North American universities
to consolidate and, by the mid-2030s, close humanities
departments.*

While these facts are easily accessible to any casual
reader, they do not do justice to what we have come
to see as a tale of professional disappointment and
spiritual conversion. For most of us today think that
"history" means an assemblage of dates, names, and

events. Because everything that happens is recorded in the Cloud, our historians are the algorithms that register all phenomena, statements, and decisions. Yet we have consulted the historical scholarship of the late twentieth century and feel humbled in the face of such writing's disciplined reliance on "primary sources," the receipts and letters and manifests and inventories and diary entries from which any decent history might (then) have been constructed. Such documents were critical for historians because history itself was contentious, not unambiguous as it is today. We, by contrast, have only the dates and facts, which are uncontroversial. We regret our incapacity to cope with controversy.

Yet we have been fortunate beyond any reckoning in finding Trent's memoir, which harkens back to an era like Gibbon's, when history read like novels and novels were histories of conflicted hearts. Trent relied on Gibbon as a model of what a historian should do: render a story whose ending we already knew into a war between half-spoken inclinations. We know who the Eddans were, what they did for and to the university. We know who Annika Trent was. But until we found Trent's memoir, we lacked insight into her actions and internal contradictions. What follows, to the best of our knowledge, fairly represents the missteps of Trent and the Eddan Collective. Thus, our decision to publish this obscure autobiographical text is our best effort to chart how one Eddan member who so passionately loved humanistic inquiry became the instrument of its undoing.

In those rare moments when we speak of the university as it used to be, a physical site of learning, it is easy to be incredulous. Why would students choose to go to study *at an institution*, when it is clearly easier and cheaper to access class practica and materials on the Cloud? We naturally excuse those who lived in

2

the 2010s and earlier, before the Cloud was universally accessible. The physical university passed away, so we say today, as a consequence of the shift toward a more perfect union with the Cloud. "Universities" are now exclusively industrial research laboratories; these are centers of applied inquiry into matters of engineering, health, science, or safety, and they depend on corporate support. But there are no more universities in the nineteenth- or twentieth-century sense of the word. For those just finishing high school, there are networks of Cloud courses on any conceivable subject. For the past two hundred years, there has been no physical university because there has been no need or desire for one. The learner need simply watch tutorials that are taught by artificial intelligence, or, in rare cases, that use video footage of lectures given by human experts long since deceased.

This explanation naturalizes a history far less logical than it may sound. The university did not pass away because it was suddenly perceived as no longer necessary, but rather because those who believed in its importance defended it in the wrong manner. Those who aspired to be the university's protectors were in fact its destroyers.

But first, the facts: the Eddan Collective was a multi-disciplinary unit of faculty researchers employed at the University of X. Many of the terms used in this history, like "multi-disciplinary" and "unit," will have little meaning for present-day readers. Suffice to say that the Eddans were founded amid deep skepticism about the future of Capitalism. The Eddans' initial mandate was to critique Capitalism and propose alternatives to it. Money, honors, recognition, and paranoia befell the group, which splintered into two factions, one that proclaimed that Capitalism was nothing less than the inevitable final stage of biological development, and the other that veered off into esotericism. Administrators who were unsympathetic to the goals of the Eddans seized on these divisions as an opportunity to assimilate the humanities at the University of X into other departments. Once those first few steps were taken, it took no great effort to close first the University of X and then universities across North America as physical sites of learning.

But all of this is jumping ahead in the story. The Eddan Collective was founded at the instigation of Annika Trent (1986–2038). Trent was an American historian and professor at the University of X, where she researched and taught classes on late Antiquity. She was instrumental in historicizing the Eddan Collective, or "the Eddans" as she called it. Upon opening an archive for the group in 2035, she deposited much of her own correspondence and personal journal entries from her period of involvement, as well as a handwritten manuscript for her unpublished memoir. Trent will have ample opportunity in the coming pages to tell us more about herself, so we turn to her main collaborator, Syd Niall (1972–2043), a professor of geology at the University of X. Niall was born and raised in Adelaide, Australia, the son of a French mother and an English father. He left Australia at the age of twenty when he moved first to England to study history at Cambridge, then to Stanford University in Palo Alto to pursue a Ph.D. in geology, which he earned in 2005. That year, Niall was hired as Assistant Professor in Earth Sciences at the University of X; he was promoted to Associate Professor with tenure (i.e., guaranteed permanent employment) in 2011. When Niall joined the group that eventually would be known as the Eddans in late 2016, he could easily have continued on the career path that seemed assured for him. With publications appearing at a steady clip, a busy research platform, and three externally-funded doctoral students, he would likely have been recognized as an international leader in his field even without the events of 2018. But Niall's star rose even further following his timely prediction of the March 2, 2018 earthquake, the epicenter of which was located near Palmdale on the San Andreas Fault. The temblor caused several hundred fatalities and $40 billion in damage. Niall's lab warned local and state authorities two hours ahead of the quake, which enabled hospitals to put their intensive care units on auxiliary power without interruption of care. The area within a ten-mile radius of Diablo Canyon nuclear power plant was notified, allowing the evacuation of personnel and nearby residents. Mass transit throughout the LA basin was suspended in preparation, and cellphone users received text messages warning against driving. Niall's team predicted a disaster, and averted a far worse catastrophe. Niall was awarded a MacArthur "genius" award in 2019, and was also promoted to Professor with an endowed chair. In the coming years, he received substantial grants from the National Science Foundation and Jet Propulsion Laboratories.

The subsequent memoir will fill in any remaining gaps in this history. But the looming question is why the Center of Humanistic Study should even bother to publish this memoir, or discuss the passing of the post-Cold War American university. We are not so naïve as to believe in the permanence of institutions. Groups, like nations and people, come and go. What rivets us to this particular history is that the university was a utopian institution, arrogant and idealistic enough to believe that it could study everything. It was frequently called the Ivory Tower. And like other famous towers, it fell as a result of its hubris and internal weaknesses. The Eddan Collective was a particularly acute strain of utopian thought, and its heightened ambitions only facilitated the university's decline and fall.

Still, we cannot help but feel some modicum of regret at not living during the era of the university. For while they aspired to understand everything, universities readily admitted that the world eludes total comprehension. We in the twenty-third century, however, do know everything, or at least everything that is worth knowing. It has not brought us satisfaction.

CHAPTER ONE
Stasis Is Form

ALL IS FAR. THE TRACES OF SNOW NEAR the top of the black fjords. The blue sky, shining and hard; no traces of yellow or orange behind that blue as there are in lower latitudes. And all is close. The red paint, flaking off from the siding of the little house that is a stone's throw from the fjord. This is where I now live, body and soul, and where my soul lived for so many years, separated from a body that lived despite itself, so far away, in the rusting sunlight. Now I am whole, at one and atoning for my missteps. The energy here flows upwards from the earth. I am just one conduit among others: the kelp processing plant, the restaurant and market, the hill above town, the children's reading glasses I once found in the field. We are all branches that hum barely audibly in sympathy with the earth.

It was my folly to believe that we could live as branches rooted to the Earth's energy. Le Pendu is strung up by his foot, a symbol of submission to unknowable forces. But he is hung upside down from trees, until he becomes one of the trees. I used to think that we needed to become like Le Pendu by turning ourselves upside down, by turning that which we avoided into that which we sought: growth downward, finding roots, renouncing the economy of time. Le Pendu in some tarot decks is sticking his tongue out. In the Viéville tarot, he smiles faintly. The upside-down orientation of the number XII on the card even suggests that Le Pendu is not hanging upside down, but rather levitating right side up even though the world around him is inverted. So I preached to the Eddans that our guide was Le Pendu, that we must become like trees, that we must overturn the inverted world.

This is a pretty way to explain events that, for the most part, were neither pretty nor ugly. Most of the players involved were well-intentioned toward others, and all believed that they were doing what was best, for themselves and, I suppose, for the University of X. The moments that demarcate historical periods trace a decline, but one that results in mediocrity and passivity. There are no barbarians at the gate.

My name is Annika Trent, and I spent my career teaching at the University of X in Los Angeles. I am an expert in late Antiquity, specifically the western half of the Roman Empire from the fourth through the sixth centuries. I chose this research area because the fall of the Roman Empire fascinated me as a young girl. The melodrama of clashing civilizations appealed to my taste for fatalistic battles. In college, I studied revisionist theories that the Empire's supposedly precipitous fall was rather a gradual letdown, often peaceful or uneventful, and at times, even an ascent rather than decline. I recall the first time I read Augustine's *City of God*, which castigated the pagan Romans who fled the invading Christian barbarians. Those thugs may have torn down and raped and stole, but they feared God enough not to defile churches. My intellectual coming-of-age was dictated by theories of the relativity of human culture, and I gradually learned to feel contempt for my childhood ideas of decline and fall. The supposed victims of Rome's collapse were pagans who acted barbarously, and the putative barbarians worshiped the Christian God of compassion. Things became less dramatic and simpler, and the magic bled out of my world. And this dissipation of wonder affected other areas of my life. I was raised Catholic, and as a young girl, I was pious enough; but as my parents chafed against the casual kitsch of post-Vatican II ecumenism, I stopped going to church, and cycled between atheism, agnosticism, and a bland New Ageism.

One vestigial belief I could not shake, my professors' efforts notwithstanding, was that the United States was in decline. The American Empire lasted a bit beyond two centuries and already seemed doomed, while the Roman Empire had remained vigorous well into its fourth century. My early beliefs about Rome's collapse did not disappear altogether, but simply transferred themselves to the present. It was now America that was faced with invaders: immigrants legal and illegal, hostile foreign influences, hackers, rival empires. Roman lead plumbing, supposedly a cause for the intellectual decline of its citizens, found its analog in our fast food and sedentary lifestyles and pollution and addiction. Roman orgies and decadence were akin to American narcissism, materialism, and moronic entertainment. It took little effort to associate the distant past with something close and familiar and real.

But numerous as the parallels between ancient Rome and contemporary America were, Rome was not a capitalist economy. Rome was mercantile, to be sure, and depended on slave labor. But it was not capitalist because its means of production hadn't yet assumed the mass scale of the industrial era, and because there were no capitalists who owned those means of production. Capitalism thus struck me as a malefic unknown. In a morbid desire to understand America's decline, I read Karl Marx for the first time, at the age of thirty. Such an admission may elicit no particular response in future readers, so let me clarify that for humanities professors starting out in the early twenty-first century, Marx was the very air we breathed, the foundation of our practice of critiquing all human institutions. However ubiquitous Marxist thought was, though, fewer and fewer among us read books to their completion.

Academia was full of leftists, but rarely did they read Marx's critique in its original form, only critiques of that critique. And after reading the first few pages of the first volume of *Capital*, I deplored my own training as an historian, a training that took Marx so much for granted that it relegated him to the odd, albeit deferential, footnote. Marx may have studied eras after the Roman Empire, but his methodology was sound, drawing on the municipal documents and newspapers and analyses that distinguish excellent research. He was a Hegelian, and my dimly remembered freshman philosophy course taught me that Hegelians broke history up into periods. So, our present descent was the inevitable result of past movements and affinities stretching back through the infancy of Capitalism, if not further. It is one thing to master one's official field of study, which, like long-term solitude, becomes comfortable and familiar over time. It is quite another to learn a new field in midlife, before learning has become impossible but well after it has ceased to be easy. I took to Marxism with the awkward eagerness of a spinster who receives her first kiss in middle-age. My eagerness was spurred by love for Marx, and also the feeling that neither the United States nor I had much time left.

I was diagnosed with an auto-immune condition at the age of seventeen, a "neoplasm of unknown provenance," as it was explained to me. The disease has no proper name, because it exhibits the symptoms of multiple diseases: the inflammation of lupus, the hematopoiesis of leukemia, the constitutional impairment of myelofibrosis. One oncologist told me when I was twenty-six that I would likely not live past my thirties. When I questioned him, he simply said that my body was fighting with itself, and couldn't decide how best to die. The medications then available were palliative only, and would not slow progression. My face is routinely flushed, and my cheeks and upper lip have always looked as if I had a sunburn. I am sweaty and bloated. My bones often ache. No one has ever thought of me as beautiful. Love has come to me by other means, in the writings of those long since dead, in untapped potential and unrealized hope. Marx made me fall in love with hope at an age when it is no longer seemly to fall in love. By comparison, Rome's problems became slighter, its fall less precipitous, because it was not subject to the crippling burden of Capitalism. And so, within the span of time it took to read volume one of *Capital*, I went from enjoying the luxury of not believing in anything, to believing passionately in a utopia disavowed by history and facts. I became a virgin Marxist.

I have the temperament of a joiner, but the chronically ill tend to isolate themselves. I knew that there would be no Marxist groups at the University of X, a nominally liberal institution that was nonetheless circumspectly funded by the defense and entertainment industries. So I started my own Marxist group, hoping that it would attract perhaps a few members and last perhaps a few months before interest died off. Academic initiatives usually do not live very long, and I entertained no illusions about my club's "impactfulness," that horrid word invented to tart up the ideal of relevance. I played with a few ideas in my mind before settling on a name, The Center for Critical Studies of Capitalism. We later became known as the Eddan Collective, or simply the Eddans.

I sent an email on 5 November 2016 to as many professors as I could find who seemed even remotely interested in Capitalism or philosophy or history. The subject heading read, "Critical Studies of Capitalism—working group." "Dear colleagues," the email began, "the election is in four days. Are you feeling hopeless? Please come to an organizational meeting on Friday, 11 November 2016, at 11:00 a.m. in Kessel 202, if you are interested in an alternative. The working title of this group is 'Critical

Studies in Capitalism,' but we can figure out the details as we go." I received no responses, but three people showed up: Joanna Demers, Leta Hugh, and Syd Niall.

The morning of the meeting, I lay in bed awake, waiting for the alarm to sound. I half-dreamt, half-imagined the earth as a Petri dish, pink and empty at the moment when one branch of hominids veered off to become what we call *Homo sapiens*. Then, that Petri dish became overcrowded and soiled, gray and brown and black. I remembered that, during my first year at university, I was briefly interested in progressive ecology. A CALPIRG volunteer convinced me to stop and talk to him rather than hurrying to Latin class. He rattled off six reasons why sustainable growth was an attainable goal. He made me a believer for all of three weeks—until I took a new history class called "Historical Ecologies," which examined the pollution in ancient Athens and Rome. The detachment of the Stoics dispelled my vaguely hoped-for perpetuation of our postwar fairytale. The ancient world was putrid, excremental, and contagious, much more than our own. Any conception of life entails an end to that life. It is born, lives for span of time, and then perishes. If this is true of animals and humans, of ideologies and ecosystems and natural phenomena and even planets, then it is surely also true of economic systems. My next conversation with the CALPIRG volunteer ended quickly. He walked away with a red face.

I showed up at the meeting a half-hour ahead of time with Styrofoam cups, a thermos of coffee, and a box of powdered donuts. Joanna Demers showed up first and was followed by Leta Hugh. Syd Niall came at five past and apologized for being late. My voice trembled when I said, "Uh, well, hello, good morning, thank you all for showing up. My name is Annika Trent, and I teach in History. Maybe we could go around the room and introduce ourselves. Well, I just did." I laughed slightly.

"Joanna Demers, Musicology. I'm interested in philosophy and especially in a return to Hegel."

"Leta Hugh, Visual Arts. I do music and sound. I'm new to the University of X, too."

Everyone offered their welcomes.

"Syd Niall, Geology. My side research project has to do with affinities between Capitalism and metabolism."

That sentence stopped me dead in my tracks, given my dream that morning. I took a sip of water before continuing. "There are plenty of Marxist clubs and reading groups throughout the world—plenty, that is, once you leave our campus." Everyone chuckled. "Although I want very much for us to keep Marx close and central," and I internally winced for making that decision for the group without consulting its members, "I think that we could bring something new to the enterprise of Marxism by using concrete academic research, not just theory, to investigate alternatives to Capitalism."

Joanna and Leta nodded sympathetically. Syd frowned, and then said, "First of all, I'm thrilled that someone has taken it upon herself to propose this group, and I would like to participate. My research platform is sympathetic to this stated goal." He hadn't even referred to me directly, only in the third person. I braced myself for the negative conjunction I knew was coming. And there it was: "But I am testing a hypothesis that, if shown to be true, would categorically refute your goal." At least he was now talking to me.

"Are you at liberty to elaborate?" I tried to keep my voice from shaking.

"Briefly: I am attempting to demonstrate that Capitalism is a natural and advanced stage of metabolism—of the metabolism of a civilization, if you will."

I exhaled. Fortunately, Leta responded first.

"Wow, that sounds like really interesting work. Are you able to conduct this research in the Geology department?"

He smiled at her. "No, my day job is predicting earthquakes." We all laughed, and the tension abated.

"I don't see that Syd's hypothesis and Annika's goals would make collaboration impossible," Joanna said. "They share a deep dissatisfaction with the experiences of late Capitalism. At least I presume that that's the case. Is that a fair statement, Syd?"

"I would say so."

All eyes turned toward mine. I was supposed to say something that demonstrated leadership. But my mind was a blank, and I fell back on what I had planned to say at the conclusion of the meeting. It was barely 11:15 a.m.

"We could select a reading that cuts diagonally, that addresses inevitability while demanding an alternative." The three of them nodded. "Perhaps Marx on the declining rate of profit?" Leta and Joanna nodded with enthusiasm, while Syd indicated a modicum of agreement. "I can scan and send the exact sections tonight."

I don't remember much else about the meeting. It deteriorated into a postmortem of the recent election. Leta mentioned her upcoming album, and Joanna already knew and admired her music. Syd looked at his watch at 11:30, and begged off to another meeting. I pretended to keep busy for the rest of the day, never shaking off the sense that I had embarked on territory for which I was unprepared. But that night Syd sent the three of us a brief message: "Thanks again for today. I apologize for being a wet blanket. Here is more on that metabolism idea. Looking forward — Syd." Four documents were attached. The first was an inventory of all the passages in *Capital*, vol. 1 in which Marx deploys biological metaphors. The second contained two graphs: one that showed growth, plateau, and decline of the US economy between 1790 and 2016, extrapolating into the future as far as 2030; the other showing the two phases of metabolic function: anabolism, or building up, and catabolism, or breaking down. He included at the bottom a superimposition of the two graphs. The contour of the metabolic curve mirrored that of every cycle in US economic history. Syd's third document was a précis on the phenomenon of axial precession, whereby Earth's axis of rotation moves in a circle around the ecliptic pole. One precessional cycle takes around 26,000 years. The fourth attachment contained four images of a Petri dish, each successive one with more black and less pink, with black filth overrunning the last dish.

There was nothing else to be done that evening, nothing other than going over the meeting and Syd's documents. I lay down in bed and, with eyes open, sent myself to a place where I could look at Syd unabashedly. He tried to evade my gaze, but I forced him to look back at me. Even then he did not see me. His eyes may have been looking outward, but they were attending to interior recriminations. I asked him, "Aren't you guilty?" He shrugged, then rolled over as if in bed, though I had thought he was standing, and then climbed on the back of a dragon that buried itself deep into the earth.

Since early childhood, I have had the ability to send myself away. That has been my way of putting it, although others have more mystical ways of expressing this action. As I was to discover only well into adulthood, it is apparently a special skill. But I thought of it merely in the no-nonsense terms of Hermes Trismegistus, who told his acolyte,

Consider this for yourself: command your soul to travel to India, and it will be there faster than your command. Command it to cross over to the ocean, and again it will quickly be there, not as having passed from place to place but simply as being there. Command it even to fly up to heaven, and it will not lack wings. Nothing will hinder it,

not the fire of the sun, nor the aether, nor the swirl nor the
bodies of the outer stars. Cutting through them all, it will
fly to the utmost body. But if you wish to break through the
universe itself and look upon the things outside (if, indeed,
there is anything outside the cosmos), it is within your power.

Sending myself away had never been something special or esoteric. I only learned later that most people cannot send themselves away. But it did become a practice indispensable to my health once I arrived at the University of X. Sometimes, as in this first instance with Syd, I set out to see a specific person or accomplish some goal. More often, however, I sent myself away simply to leave. My destination was usually the Icelandic village, Bíldudalur. I first traveled there, body and soul together, when I went with a few college friends to Iceland the summer I turned twenty-two. We had spent eight hours driving one interminable day, from Akureyri on the north-central coast, to the northwest fjords. I was in a rotten mood with the driving and my companions' tired jokes and exclamations over the beautiful scenery. We limped into town by eight in the evening, the early-summer sun nowhere near setting.

Our lodgings for the night consisted of a little red house that, along with the rest of the town, was nestled in a corner of the fjord. The population must not have exceeded a hundred residents. It was not a tourist destination, and its two salient features were a processing plant for kelp and a museum of sea monsters. The house was modest and clean and felt like the 1970s vacation home for a family of average means. The owner, a woman in her mid-20s, said that she had lived in Bíldudalur all her life. The fixtures and knobs, flooring and spiral staircase all bespoke an effortless happiness, not caring whether there were sufficient grounds for such happiness. If I had stayed there for longer than the one night we had planned, I knew that I could be capable of writing a novel or a book of poetry. The scenery and the town perched on oblivion's edge compelled me to return again and again, and so I made a habit out of sending myself back to Bíldudalur. At first, it was merely to recall the details of my visit, although there wasn't much to recollect: just our ill-tempered arrival; our spaghetti dinner made in the red house's simple kitchen; sleeping on the upper floor where the ceiling was dangerously low; feeling a maddening rush of possibility in this place forgotten by the rest of the planet; driving the next morning into a fog complicit with the village's desire for solitude. My trips to Bíldudalur gradually assumed other guises. I went there at times simply for rest and solace, drinking coffee while sitting at the window that looked out over the water. The living room became a studio where I could write in peace, without the distractions of a computer or telephone. There, I wrote the poetry I had known was in me but that was hiding stubbornly beneath the impediments of routine and distraction. I imagined parties there with guests living or dead, real or fictional: Edward Gibbon, Samuel Johnson, Marguerite Porete, Captain Francis Crozier, Quentin Compson, Plotinus, St. Faustina Kowalska.

My sending myself away to Syd was therefore nothing new, but it lacked the comfort that a visit to Bíldudalur would have provided. As I drifted off to sleep, I scoped the earth beneath me for dragons, for idealists who became cynics. The earth is a tight place. It is not enough to say that it is cold or dark. It is crowded and lonely, fit more for those who can turn the solid into air, like Marx.

After several days of hesitation, I finally drummed up the nerve to send Syd a message, and we met for coffee.

"If what you hypothesize is true," I began once we sat down and got through pleasantries, "if Capitalism is inherent to the development of life, then it doesn't sound as if we have much choice in the matter."

"Ah, well, choice is overrated, now, isn't it?" He acted differently from how he had been in the meeting—more relaxed, and even possessing a sense of humor.

"But what can we do?"

"I hadn't really thought about it, to be honest. There's so much to investigate already that I hadn't permitted myself the luxury of imagining the next steps."

"Sure, but what do we do if you do prove that link? If we are content to do nothing, then we embrace the worst sort of biological determinism."

"Why?" His smile was gone, and he looked at me almost aggressively. "Why do you say 'the worst sort'? I don't really understand why biological determinism should be something to loathe."

I became so exasperated that I didn't know how to respond. "We should just accept all of our basest animal impulses, then? To kill and rape?"

"That's where you're wrong. Those aren't 'base animal impulses.' They are behaviors that were adapted to certain contexts earlier in history. But the benefits of society are so great that they justify suppressing those behaviors. Behaviors are subject to natural selection as much as physical characteristics."

"Then what do you conceive as biologically determined, if we can change our behavior?"

"There are certain constants, yeah? Not many, but a few—the need for oxygen, water, food. The desire to survive and reproduce. Those are nonnegotiable."

"So is Capitalism an expression of the desire to survive?"

"Not 'an' expression. It's the only expression. All species get there, sooner or later, if they persist long enough."

He didn't mind my arguments. To the contrary, he seemed relieved to speak openly, but he was entirely unmoved. And what I searched for, the idealistic core beneath the cynical shell, was nowhere to be seen.

But then his demeanor changed slightly, as if he had resigned himself to indulging me. "We can certainly address the question of 'what then?' In order to do so, we'd of course need to flesh out the contention that Capitalism is a symptom of metabolism. We will need to look at rates: rates of growth, rates of consumption. In my field, we study processes that do not accelerate over any significant period of time. Precession, for instance, is cyclical. And other geological phenomena exhibit stasis, or else a rate of change so slow that it might as well be stasis when compared to a human lifespan. So maybe the potential for agency can be found in deriving models that do something other than indicate increasing rates of demand, or declining rates of profit."

He sipped his coffee and checked his phone as I searched for something to say.

"It'd be hard, going against everything we are programmed to want," I said finally.

"How do you mean?"

"We all grow. And growth patterns often feature brief moments of acceleration—growth spurts. As we become sexually mature, a good deal of our thought and energy is spent plotting reproduction, another type of growth. But deceleration and retraction run counter to our desires. They are phenomena that, for us, indicate aging and death, things we tend to avoid as much as possible."

"We'd have to learn another way of being." It was one of the only times I would hear him say something poetic.

I asked him to tell me about his research. "Ah, you mean, how did a nice geologist like me get caught up in Marxism?" Syd went on to say that he specialized in detecting and predicting seismic activity. He belonged to a consortium of scientists from Caltech, Japan, and

Iceland that were developing early-warning systems for earthquakes and volcanic eruptions. As an undergrad at Cambridge, Syd had a secondary field in the history of economics. He regarded geology and economics both as fields that predict catastrophe.

"What struck me when I left the UK was how few people actually read Marx."

"I know what you mean," I gushed. "I only started reading him a year ago."

He went on as if he hadn't heard me. "Of course, most scientists wouldn't need to read him. But humanists—literature professors, historians, philosophers, artists—although they may reference Marx in talking about postmodernism, they don't actually work with him."

"They let Adorno do that."

"Or Althusser, or Žižek!" He smiled. I seemed to have said something witty. "There's too much to read, and every year we all add heaps to the pile. No one can grasp it all. So why not let the older stuff go? Others have already reported on it." He sighed and the smile faded. "That's what some people think, at any rate."

"This is surprising to hear, coming from a scientist."

"Is it?" he said absently, his mind on the text he was now answering. Once he put down his phone, he looked off at the milling students and continued, "Research academia has boxed itself into a corner. In fact, it's exactly the same predicament as the one into which Capitalism has fallen. There are too many of us, too much research to read, more and more being published every year. Resisting that flow is a futile gesture, to paraphrase *Star Trek*. But acquiescing to it usually entails the decision to leave out the older stuff, the boring stuff, the books too big to read. Why read Marx when Wikipedia tells you what you need to know in a few minutes? Especially if it frees up time to study trans disabled Chicano lit."

His comment made me freeze for what seemed like an eternity to ask myself questions, each of which escalated my anxiety. Why would he say such clearly actionable things to me, a stranger? Was he too oblivious to understand the danger? Was he a bigot? Did he *want* me to know that he was a bigot? Or was this another example of a tenured white male professor feeling overconfident? Or (and here is where time ground to a halt in my mind) was this a surreptitious, and certainly clumsy, even stupid, means of conveying his trust or even liking of me? Did he already feel comfortable enough to let down his guard to show me the "true" Syd, the one not beaten down by mandatory unconscious bias prevention trainings? Was this the beginning of intimacy between us?

"We widen the gap between ourselves and the past with each passing year." I veered toward the inoffensive abstract, almost sure that his indiscretion was a veiled signal that he wanted more from our relationship.

"Which is a particularly vexing situation for historians like you." He smiled. "So it's up to those of us who are so inclined to practice an archaeology of epistemology. We don't know all that much about how people of the past thought. Oh, we think we know their theories and belief systems. But we read secondary literature, which is a professional *Reader's Digest*," his voice dripped with disgust, "about the past. It's more important to know what some English professor at Berkeley has to say about Marx than it is to know what Marx wrote."

"That's often true, though not always. But what do you and I and our colleagues do after we've read Marx? Your hypothesis has stark ramifications." I listened to myself, to how calm I sounded. "You dare to suggest that our biological programming compels us to become capitalist. The wrong type of student will conclude that there's nothing to be done but to embrace Capitalism. So we must have in our right hand an alternative, even as we offer your diagnosis in our left." I spoke with the awkward syntax of someone who had only recently started to learn English.

"You're right." He stopped before saying what I wanted to hear, some palliative that would have offered consolation. Although in other respects he seemed a thoroughly political animal, some weakness or blind spot prevented him from furnishing the pretty words that would smooth over an awkward silence. "And that's why I need help. I need to know what I haven't yet learned, what I need to care about."

"And that is why you are bothering with my little club," I said. It would have been appropriate for him to smile and deny any such condescension. He could have flattered my initiative, and declared his enthusiasm for the project. He did none of those things. His eyes passed over me before he checked his messages again. His crude joke was nothing other than a crude joke, and I left the café, more troubled than before.

The few remaining weeks of that semester passed quickly. Syd, Leta, Joanna, and I had agreed on the next meeting taking place in early January. So it was a pleasant surprise to see Leta in December. I was on the mailing list of the Visual Arts Department, which held a retrospective of student and faculty work at the end of each semester. I made it a habit of attending these events. Spending my time with undergraduate students who usually submitted projects at the last minute and who displayed an aversion toward writing, it was inspiring to see the work of these art students who seemed genuinely to enjoy their work.

The quality of the student projects that night was high as usual. I recall little about them, probably because my attention was riveted to the last work on the program, a video piece by none other than Leta.

It was in black and white and, as far as I could tell, was shot first on film before being transferred to digital format. The filmic qualities reminded me of the screenings from barely functional projectors used at my elementary school so many years before. Dust, electrical current variations, and the brittleness of the film created a throbbing quality of the light, which pulsated in a regular and nearly lifelike rhythm. The image was difficult to discern; it could have been abstract shapes or objects in a circle, or else topological features as seen from midair.

But where the footage by itself could have quickly become stale or monotonous, the musical accompaniment imbued it with pathos. It was lo-fi, with a single electric guitar line playing a simple eight-bar melody in its low register. There was luxuriant reverb almost to the point of becoming echo, and the blurry playback quality suggested several iterations of tape dubbing, as if this had been a homemade tape copied three or four times from the original. So the image and music were both cyclical, and while I briefly feared that there would be some final deviation, some definitive concluding statement writ large, the rhythm and content proceeded undeterred. The title of the work was "Stasis Is Form."

I looked for Leta afterward and caught up to her as she was being congratulated by a host of people, including Syd. Although the stars of this sort of soirée were the students, Leta was clearly a jewel of her department. She smiled at me quickly even as her eyes searched mine. It lasted only a split second and she hid it well, but it was clear that she didn't recognize me. No matter, I thought, it's hard to remember faces when seen out of context. She had so much on her mind that evening, anyway. Her black hair was swept up into a bun, and a few strands had already escaped and framed her face. She wore a navy blue mini-dress and black stockings. The light in her eyes and the white of her skin, the dark red of her fingernail polish, and the silver sprinkles on her high-top sneakers — all recalled the droplets that fell from the heavens in the Moon tarot card. I barely had time to murmur my congratulations before someone came from behind me to enfold Leta in a bear hug.

At home, I prepared a list of questions for Leta. But I thought better of it, and simply sent myself to her: a dark place crowded with stars and water droplets, floating rather than falling. But that fragile light flashed and fluttered like eyelids struggling in blinding light. That light was from the alternation of day with night in absurd oscillation. The moon alone traced some line of sense, varying with its waxing to fullness and waning to darkness. The moon alone was stable and calm amid this insane clip. I found Leta who was sitting on the grass with her two dogs just above the coast. Crustaceans of unknown provenance were moving in the dark water, surfacing intermittently to snap their pincers and then retreat into the water. Leta turned to me and, smiling, said, "Stasis is form."

"Yes, but how is it that time is moving so quickly?"

"Stasis is form."

"But nothing here is static."

"Yes. That is the stasis."

The moon's transits across the sky continued. A pattern eventually emerged from their circuits, a pattern that took twelve or thirteen cycles to perceive. There was stasis amid the movement, stasis that supported the chaos. The night and floating droplets, the dogs and crabs, their chatter and movement gradually congealed into a plastic calm, a softness that enclosed all objects, ideas, and cares. The dogs howled at the moon. The crabs scurried back and forth underwater. Leta smiled at me even as her beautiful face grew wrinkled.

CHAPTER TWO
As You Were

IN AD 410 THE VISIGOTH CHIEF ALARIC invaded Rome, and over the ensuing decade Gothic and Vandal troops overran much of what remained of the Roman Empire.

With just this one sentence, I have likely conjured in your mind a thrilling drama in which unwashed barbarian hordes overpower the one remaining beacon of civilization. It's a persistent vision, this myth of the war between cultures, worlds, and gods. But Alaric, who otherwise behaved like a conqueror in sacking cities and slaughtering enemies, was himself a devout Arian Christian commanding thousands of Christian soldiers. He ordered that Christian churches in Rome be treated as inviolable sanctuaries. Alaric's soldiers were obliged to spare all who had sought shelter in church, whether they happened to be Christian or not. Many Roman pagans sought refuge in these churches. Those who were well-off later fled across the Mediterranean to North Africa. And once they were out of immediate danger, some of those pagan refugees placed blame for the invasions on Christianity—not on human avarice, but rather a religion of love and mercy. Then, as today, culpability was a complicated affair.

St. Augustine, Bishop of Hippo, was born in AD 354. He was ethnically Punic (similar to the Berbers of today), but his mother tongue was Latin. He grew up in the fertile agricultural coastal region of what is now Algeria, the son of a respected family, a well-educated boy in a land of farmers. He was pagan until early adulthood, despite the tears and prayers of his devoutly Catholic mother, Monica. He loved reading and philosophy, and briefly flirted with Manichaeism. He worked as a schoolteacher. He lived with a woman who was not his wife and had a son with her. He traveled to Milan and Rome where he studied with the famous Ambrose, Bishop of Milan. Incredibly, Monica's prayers were eventually answered, and around the time he turned thirty, Augustine began the process of conversion to Catholicism. His son, Adeodatus, a teenager, also converted. After Monica's death, he and Adeodatus returned to North Africa and planned to live a life of private contemplative prayer. Then, Adeodatus died unexpectedly, and the brokenhearted Augustine sold his goods, gave the money to the poor, and converted his family home to a monastery. He was ordained in 391 in Hippo, where he remained until his death.

Augustine was a prolific author of sermons and letters, his autobiography (*The Confessions*), and an enormous meditation on the end of the Roman world, *City of God*. He began writing this sprawling work three years after Alaric's invasion of Rome, and he opened the work by comparing the humanity of Gothic invaders to the indifference of the Roman vanquished. It is jarring for a modern scholar, trained to avoid cliché and hyperbole, to read Augustine's reactions to the invasion. Augustine likens Rome's fall to the fall of Troy. It is a catastrophe of literally epic proportions. And while Roman pagans blamed Roman Christians for abandoning the old protector gods of the city, Augustine retorts that it is the nature of human institutions and cities to fall. Christianity, rather than being party to the collapse of Rome, provided the path to a perfect city of permanence, the City of God. This dialectical relationship between the ideal and the mundane is the underlying concept of *City of God*. For Augustine describes two cities: the

Earthly City of Rome, once presumed impregnable but now shown to be rotting from the inside out; and the Celestial City of God, the Jerusalem of the soul that remains inviolate for faithful believers. Augustine's argument is thus a Platonic gesture, for the world delivered to our senses is transient and willfully misleading. That which lasts and is real is the other realm, of the cross and faith, of chalices and quests and three red drops of blood on white snow. Augustine died just as another barbarian tribe, the Vandals, was laying siege to Hippo. He passed away before the Vandals entered and their King Geiseric made Hippo the capital of the Vandal kingdom. I used to wonder what Augustine would have said about Geiseric, who, like Alaric, was an Arian and therefore a heretic in the eyes of Catholics. Geiseric was a true believer in Arianism, but tolerant enough to permit African lay Catholics to practice their faith. Yet he imposed heavy taxes on the rich as well as the Catholic liturgy. Would Augustine have favored Geiseric's heresy over Roman indifference, the tepidness that made him complain to his countrymen, "When, by all accounts, nations in the East were bewailing your catastrophe, when the greatest cities in the farthest parts of the earth were keeping days of public grief and mourning, you were asking the way to the theatres, and going in, making full houses . . ."?

Only a few months after invading the City of Rome, Alaric continued southward into Calabria, fell ill, and died. His men buried him with a vast amount of plundered treasure under a river bed. A river was temporarily redirected to permit interment, and then allowed to reenter its normal channel. Augustine, as mentioned above, died just as the Vandals were attacking Hippo in 430. King Geiseric lived long past them both, dying in his old age in 477 after having subdued Rome and most of the Western Mediterranean. My doctoral adviser wrote the definitive biography of

Augustine twenty years before I entered graduate school. In attending seminars and listening to my adviser, I was inculcated with the feeling that Augustine was a venerable ancestor only recently deceased. Anecdotes gave him life and depth, and he was far more human than the images of him on stained-glass windows and illuminated manuscripts would suggest. These details of his life became like family genealogies that, when properly consulted, would explain everything I would ever need to understand about the rise and fall of empires, or religious conversion, or the burdens of administrative work.

During the winter of 2017, it was difficult not to succumb to the Left's hysteria following Trump's election. I did my best, though, through avoiding colleagues as much as possible. When meetings required our mutual attendance, I kept the conversation on work. The rift that isolated me from those around me was widening. My peers seemed to want to pin the blame for everything that was going wrong on Trump. But few Leftists saw Trump for what he was, the fruition of the internal contradictions of late Capitalism. I had already become certain of the imminent collapse of Capitalism, compared to which the Trump presidency was just a sideshow. And, unlike my peers, I derived no pleasure from this impending fall. Augustine disabused me of any such fantasies. I had long since given up on the earthly world, and perhaps my nascent interest in Marx was at its heart just a fancy way of disguising that renunciation. But by 2017, I acquired the new habit of sending myself away to the person who could talk to me of that ideal realm, Augustine himself.

I sent myself away to him for the first time that winter. I arrived somewhat outside Hippo at the edge of an olive tree forest. It was a maze of light and odor and shadow. The sun, filtered through branches, always found its way to my eyes. It was the gold of harpsichord playing, the brittle constancy that renews itself amid confinement and decay. Upon entering the wood, it took my eyes over a minute to adjust to the darkness, and, during that minute I concluded that the light was now extinguished, that there'd be no more where I was headed. And that minute passed, and the sun returned, partitioned and schismatic because of olive arms and fingers. During that minute of blindness, I discovered for the first time my olfactory sense, which was not (as I had previously believed) a second-tier faculty, at play only as an adjunct in cooking or cleaning. In the olive grove, fragrance functioned as a sort of sonar, repelling me from one place as it drew me to another. The earth, humid and sharp, was the foundation, everywhere at the same time. Atop the earth, there were pillars of astringent, the trunks that were bitter and at times moldy. There were cooler, hermetic spheres of young, nearly sweet ripening olives. I almost didn't recognize those nascent fruits, for their scent began as something flat, almost plastic, and only upon exhalation did the suggestion of olives as I knew them arise, olives for oil, in salad, by themselves, a round and comforting glaze. Less frequent but present nonetheless were animals, their droppings and stray fur and feathers, their urine sprayed on trunks to mark territory.

And then, the shadows, the secret paradise of this grove, secret because one always begins by preferring what is light, has color and taste, and asserts its existence. Shadows harbor no such insecurities. A shadow has given up on impressing onlookers. People who seek attention will feign darkness, but a true shadow lets eyes pass over it. I had to force myself to see the shadows of branches strewn across already dark trunks and soil. Those shadows were most visible when they fell on yellow leaves that themselves had recently fallen onto the earth. They, the shadows, destroy nothing, make nothing disappear. They only attenuate.

I made my way through that forest, to Augustine's church. Even as the light in my January bedroom in Los Angeles was already in the process of dying at half past three, his little cell next to the church in Hippo was bright. The wind that wafted intermittently from the port smelled of olives and fish. The city was busy, irritated at the Roman refugees, and tense with its own divisions. Rumors abounded of an army of blond, sky-eyed marchers coming from the West, but originating from much further north and east. But the city was also alive, gawky like an adolescent still wearing a child's clothes. Augustine was lying on his cot when I appeared, staring up at the ceiling. His hands were clasped over his heart, and he was breathing in a somewhat unnatural fashion, as if he were imagining himself speaking, lips motionless but inhaling in time with his words. I could not tell if he was praying or simply envisioning what he might say, perhaps in a sermon he was planning. I sat still in a corner, careful to maintain my silence. Somehow, Augustine gradually became aware of my presence, although his body position did not change and he did not turn to look at me. His breathing slowed and became more regular, and, after a few moments, he moistened his lips as if preparing to speak. Still, he said nothing for several minutes. I did not move. Then, finally, he began:

"Why are you here?"

"I've heard so much about you. You might be the only person who could help me."

"That would be how you work."

I hesitated. "Sorry?"

"You and your kind." He inhaled shallowly and shakily, speaking slowly. "You spy on your targets before choosing which ones to assail."

"I can assure you, I'm not here to hurt you."

"That would be how you speak."

It hadn't been my intention to begin my conversation with Augustine through an argument, yet somehow we were already arguing. "I have a question to ask you. Only you can answer it. I would not trouble you otherwise."

He said nothing, gazing upwards, blinking from time to time.

"Is there change in the City of God?"

He chuckled a bit, then said, "A funny manner to trick me into blasphemy. Your kind hasn't tried that yet."

"I do not blaspheme, and I do not want to lead you to blasphemy either."

"No, for you serve a lord who regards blasphemy as truth."

"My question is not meant as a trap. Although I am in every way unfit to walk in your shadow, I share one attribute with you. My city is also falling, and I attempt to help my fellow citizens choose the right path."

He had stopped snickering and was listening.

"Only, my brethren think that the right path is an uphill climb. Fighting wars against barbarians, building new edifices. Unholy ascent: everything that led us to this fall in the first place."

Augustine whispered, "Be gone, demon, and tempt me no further."

"Father, I am not a demon come to tempt you. If you must regard me as a spirit, think of me as a lost spirit from a distant land, one who has come to seek guidance from a teacher. My brethren snipe and laugh as my home crumbles. This is something you, of all people, can understand."

He began to word silently a prayer, which he repeated several times. Then, his demeanor calmed slightly, as if some new thought just occurred to him.

"You are probably a demon. Or, you may be an angel sent to test my faith. I admit to God that I cannot discern which of the two you are. Your ways are too subtle, they exceed my old mind. Both a demon and an angel could divine ideas I have not yet put in writing.

But I can answer your question, regardless of your true nature, and still remain true to Our Father. The ways of this world are always in ascension and descent. We fell with Adam, we think that we climb, but we usually fall again. Christ subjected himself to that fall in assuming the body of a man. He did so that we might follow Him in letting our bodies fall, in giving everything up, so that we might rise with Him in eternal life. But unless we follow Christ's fall, that turning of a morbid wheel will never lead to God."

"So the world's fall and rise is a cycle, a wheel?"

"You said it."

"So, nothing changes."

"We think that there is change, but our Lord shows us otherwise."

"Is the City of God also changeless?"

"Yes, forcibly. Turning away from perfection would be sinful. But who knows? Perhaps there are changes, like the seasons or tides. These do not thwart the Kingdom."

I persisted. "But then, what distinguishes the morbid wheel that turns here on Earth from any cycle in the city of God?"

I began to wonder if he had fallen asleep, for he didn't move or react for several moments. Then he said, "Heavenly cycles know their center. They turn around the Father, and will do so until the End. Worldly cycles are composed of arrivals and departures, of culmination. That is why we will never know contentment on Earth, because we mistake the wheel for a road leading somewhere away from our descent."

He paused, and then added, "You are dealing in Origenist heresy. Or, you are an angel sent to lead me out of heresy myself. I do not know yet which."

I looked out of the little window in his cell. Strident voices were arguing, perhaps haggling over merchandise or disputing theology, yet all I could see were the olive trees outside the abbey. Discord was rampant, but the city was adept at forging ahead despite its difficulties. I had reached the limit for what could be an appropriate first conversation with Augustine. Perhaps I had already exceeded that limit. His eyes were closed, and whether he was truly sleeping or only pretending, I could not tell. I inhaled and closed my eyes, and then I was on a street in the city close by, and would have been in danger of being trampled by people and carts. But I was merely a shade to those around me. I wove in and out of the crowd, sometimes walking through objects or people when there was no other choice. Some beggars had staked claims on street intersections, and next to them sat some poor souls so utterly sick that they seemed incapable even of breathing. One beggar sat cross-legged, his lap cradling the head of a small, old woman. The woman stared upwards, her mouth partially open. Flies intermittently landed on her lips, took off at the threat of the man's hand, and then returned to her mouth. Her eyes never blinked. The beggar holding her hummed to himself a little motif, only three or four pitches, repeatedly. He apparently could sense my presence though I had not intended to make myself known to him. He looked at me, or through me, with concern, humming all the while even as he moved his hands protectively around the old woman's head.

"Your mother?" I asked.

He did not react at first. But then he set to talking, and I could see that he was missing most of his bottom teeth. "I began reading seventeen years ago because I was tired of getting hauled into work gangs. People think that the worst thing about begging is the life of hunger. But that is only part of it. Soldiers have dragged me to dig ditches into which they shit and piss, while I was still digging. Citizens have dragged me into their villas to pick fruit or clean pig troughs. Brigands and drunkards have beaten me for sport. All of them beat me, sooner or later. Reading scraps of scrolls I find in refuse piles has given me better cover than I could ever have hoped for. The texts told me what I had suspected, that roads are really seas, and carts are ships, and merchants are pirates. I know more than this, too.

"So I know about you and your kind. You are here to take my mother. You are a *malayka* and you came down from heaven, and you will carry her soul to see the One Soul. You will take her to the mountain made of porphyry, where twelve maidens wait to wrap her in gauze and to sprinkle spices into her mouth and on her chest. They will anoint her lips with frankincense and touch the palms of her hands and the soles of her feet with oils. Then, you and they will carry my dear mother into the sanctuary, and at first dawn the One Soul will shine down upon her, and she will finally have arrived home."

"I am not a *malayka*." I tried to sound gentle.

"You are a *malayka* and you heard the prayers I have said every night. My mother will find peace, finally, after a life of abjection. I await another *malayka*, but she will come only after you have led my dear mother to her home. My *malayka* will take me to a different place, as deep in the ocean as my mother's porphyry mountain is high. My blessed *malayka* is dressed in green robes, and she floats so lightly in the waves, but she can drop like a stone when she wills it. She will take me by the ankles and will not let go. I will hold my breath as long as I can, and I will dread that first breath of seawater I will have no choice but to take. But the light will break out in my body with that first breath and will spread from my mouth to my lungs to my heart. I will see the stone castles at the bottom of the sea, lit with glowing lichen and silver. Handmaidens will await me, as they will have awaited my dear mother. They will perform the ablutions on me, and I will see the One Soul."

"I am not a *malayka*. You have longer to wait, I'm afraid."

The beggar gave no indication that he heard or understood my words, and I then realized that I was invisible and inaudible to him. He could merely sense my presence. All the while, he continued humming his little motif, but it was something that I recognized from an orchestra concert of contemporary music I had recently attended. His scratchy voice intoned the theme that had made me weep when I first heard it. It traced the fall of a body descending to the ocean floor, only it did so again and again, more than a dozen times. It always began the same way, with an affliction, a fear of unspoken yet certain outcomes, sitting with preordained suffering. But after that first pain, the remaining descent was calmer. I may have been imagining a sort of self-consciousness on the part of the motif, a calm stemming from knowledge that the morbid wheel was spinning and would continue to spin thus, indefinitely. Augustine said *morbid wheel*; if only he could have imagined Shakespeare's *mortal coil*. The beggar rocked slightly as he hummed, taking care not to disturb his mother. We stayed that way for some moments, and then the beggar looked down at his mother's face, which had not moved since I arrived. He closed her eyes, and brushed her forehead with his lips. He looked in my direction vaguely and, inclining his head, said, "Thank you."

I went back to walking, this time down to the docks where ships and boats of all sizes were fastened. There were galleys, dinghies, fishing vessels of varying lengths. One of the larger ships was in the process of being loaded with merchandise: a few rugs, several containers of what was probably wine or olive oil, and several women whose wrists were bound by rope. The crew was lighter-skinned than most people of the city, and the language they spoke was nothing like Latin or Greek or Coptic. The men were tall; they wore their hair long and tied in back, and their beards were braided. I sent myself to view the land from which they came: a land much colder and darker than North Africa, where women knitted by the fire and also spoke of the morbid wheel, of striving and affliction and discontent. Behind the brawn of those northern arms and accents dwelt the same terror and hunger and blindness. One of their old women threw bones before their departure several months before. The bones were inscribed with runes, and augured nothing good and nothing bad, just a voyage and some plunder and blood and then a homecoming, and then more leaving and returning once again.

I would have stayed longer with the old woman who cast runes. I may well have stayed there forever, leaving my earthly body in California to waste away. But even as I was standing by the ships in Hippo, I was drawn to think back to one of the most singular experiences of my time in graduate school, which took the form of a digression during a seminar entitled "The Private and the Public in Late Antiquity." My dissertation advisor, the preeminent biographer of Augustine, taught the seminar. On this particular day late in the fall semester, we half-dozen students were in a sullen mood. It was cold outside and all the leaves had fallen from the trees. Yet there was no snow on the ground, and the neo-gothic architecture and sky were the same slate gray. My advisor walked into the seminar room carrying a pile of books, as was his habit. He smiled kindly at us, with that manner of senior academics too old to have been bludgeoned by the recently escalating expectations for advancement in the professoriate. He was a decent man and sensitive, after a fashion, to the precariousness of the life of a young graduate student. He knew that most of us who aspired to jobs like his would be disappointed. That said, he lived none of that precariousness. He published when he felt like it, which admittedly was still often enough for him to be regarded as productive. He also breathed easily, serene in the knowledge that nothing could harm his comfortable position at one of the richest universities in the world. That serenity impelled him, as kind and sincere as he was, to occasionally bizarre behavior that unnerved those around him.

So it was on that late-autumn day that my advisor proposed an impromptu class exercise called "Diagnosis with the Greeks," a sort of mock-quiz show. And because we students were peevish and tired, we all went along with the game, grateful for anything other than the normal seminar fare. My advisor explained the rules: one student would pretend to be ill and another would pretend to be Galen, the prominent Roman physician who was a contemporary of Marcus Aurelius. This seemed like a fun game. But my advisor intended for all the creativity to stem from the "physician." The "patient" was to read symptoms from notecards my advisor had prepared in advance. My advisor announced that the first physician/patient pairing was to be my friend Wayne and me.

Wayne was a close friend, and could sense my unease with the game. I read my first lines flatly: "Hello, doctor. I suffer from something, but I don't know if it has a name. I feel tired often. My ribs hurt and my gums bleed. My hips ache." I trailed off, even though there were other lines to read. Wayne shot an agonized expression at me, but dared say nothing. My advisor gently tried to get me to say more, and when I declined, he said with some frustration, "Well, get on with it, Galen — diagnose her!"

Wayne's eyes begged forgiveness from me before he began to ventriloquize what my advisor wanted to hear: questions about my diet, my tongue color and size, my pulse, the odor of my breath, urine, and stools, the length of my menstrual cycle. But he refused to perform the actions that my advisor also expected, such as tapping my back and listening to my lungs, or depressing my exposed tongue with a popsicle stick that was probably not sterile. My advisor grew increasingly frustrated, and Wayne was about to blurt out something in exasperation, but I glared at him, and he stifled his words. My advisor read our faces and could see that there was some reason for our reticence, and he concluded audibly and indulgently that we must have stage fright. The silence in the room was becoming uncomfortable, and my advisor finally said, "If I were Galen, I would not have use of laboratories or access to the latest in medical research, but I would be able to come up with a decent, basic understanding of Annika's ills. Annika, you see, is suffering from a chronic, debilitating condition, but its progression is so slow that she might well die of old age, from other causes, before this sickness has the chance to kill her. And I chose Annika's symptoms very carefully because I wanted to put into a personal and private form the very ills that plagued the Empire by this point in history, the fourth century. Like Annika, the Empire suffers, but it too has no word to identify that suffering. Like Annika, the Empire is tired. Its defenses are weak, and it is constantly beset by aggressors. Its infrastructures are falling to pieces. Its sanitation services (in Annika's case, the spleen; in the Empire's case, the sewers) are overworked. Both Annika and the Empire might once have been vital and thriving, but today they are but shadows of their former selves."

"There is only one point on which you're mistaken, Professor," I said quietly. "I never thrived. I was born into sickness."

My advisor chuckled good-naturedly, the irony having missed him completely. In his distraction, he probably hadn't even heard what I said. Wayne and I watched the rest of the seminar as if through a glass pane, reeling that my advisor had inadvertently diagnosed my true medical condition for our fellow graduate students to see. Illness and empire were henceforth forever linked; the object of my intellectual passion had suddenly become intertwined with my private cross.

The memory had run its course and I was back standing on the dock in Hippo, gazing at the northerners and seeing through their eyes the old woman who cast runes. The old woman glanced up from her work and looked directly into my eyes. There was no doubt that she knew I was there, who I was, and how I came to be watching her. She too could speak without talking, and she told me that the runes promised nothing new, just eternity and stasis. *Like what Augustine sees?* I asked. *No*, she responded, *because your master thinks that his god is above the morbid wheel. We know better. For our god is the morbid wheel.*

The woman wasn't bothered by my presence, and we likely would have continued conversing, but a man's voice called for her from outside — "Edda," he cried, their word for "grandmother" — and she let her runes fall still to go see him. I fell back to Hippo, and then fell again to my bedroom in Los Angeles. It was as if nothing had happened.

CHAPTER THREE
Another Way of Being

"WE MUST LEARN ANOTHER WAY OF BEING" was the subject of the message I sent to the group a few days later, reminding them of our upcoming meeting in which we were to brainstorm alternatives to Capitalism. *I'm sure Marx had many such spitballing sessions with Engels,* I thought to myself. The morning of the meeting, I printed out a list of questions for distribution:

> Is there any relationship between Syd's theory (i.e., that Capitalism is a stage of metabolism) and the three laws of thermodynamics?

> If given enough time, will all lifeforms arrive at the metabolic stage known as Capitalism?

> What role does evolution play here? Do only especially evolved lifeforms reach the capitalist stage?

> Are there models in nature that could serve as *analogies* to Marx's declining rate of profit? (The purpose of the italics was to be made clear.)

> Are there models in nature that could serve as *alternatives* to Marx's declining rate of profit? (Now, the reason for italics was made manifest, for "analogies" merely maintains the status quo, while "alternatives" envisions another future.)

I was proud of the cleverness of my writing.

I sat in our designated meeting place, shuffling and straightening the handouts. Five minutes passed, and no one had arrived. By ten past, Joanna sent an email with apologies: too much work. Leta wrote at quarter past: home sick with a cold. By then I was feeling surly, for Syd hadn't even bothered to come up with an excuse, and I sent a group response with no subject heading and no message, just my questions attached.

Ten minutes later, Syd responded: "Sorry, I double-booked myself this morning. Great questions. You should come with us on Saturday. I take my first-year masters students to Pelican Cove to look for minerals. It's very user-friendly. If you want alternatives found in nature, it'd be a place to start."

It was Syd's attempt at being supportive, and I loathed myself for the eagerness with which I accepted his invitation. I met Syd and his students that Saturday at the appointed cove in Palos Verdes. The weather was cold and sunny, and although the wind blew as we stood at the top of the path, we were protected by the time we reached the beach. I had once visited this place over three decades before, when Marineland stood where the resort Terranea has since been built. I remembered the same synapse dividing what I anticipated when looking down at the cove from the cliffs, and what I in fact beheld once down at the level of the water. From above, the ocean color ranged from turquoise to midnight blue. Up close, the water was obsidian near the shore, with no trace of blue. The beach was no beach at all, but a minefield of boulders and teetering rocks. The waves went on in their merciless cycle: three weak ones followed by a fourth that sucked out the water just before crashing in again. It took me some time to realize that the low drone that waxed and waned was not highway noise from above the cliffs, but rather water infiltrating all the crevices between the pebbles, rocks, and gigantic stones. Nothing could remain a void for longer than a few seconds. This certainty was dully comforting.

Syd led us to the western point of the cove and then continued alone to a large deposit of barite crystals. I sat on one of the smooth pedestal-like stones that jutted upwards at a fifteen-degree angle. Catalina Island was clear and its valleys and summits unusually discernible, and it took up most of the horizon. The students eventually filed past me to the path leading back up to our cars, and I smiled as Syd half-heartedly offered to wait for me. "Thank you, I think I might stay on a bit," I yelled. Syd's relief was obvious; by the time I reached my car, he had already driven off. I had already sent myself away to this same place, as I had first seen it in 1990. I spent the rest of the day there, overlaying memories of trips physical and astral to what was happening in the present moment. I had vertigo, but that didn't matter. This was the alternative. The cycle overcame the decline, or, rather, decline was only one part of the cycle. Everything in the cove manifested the cycle: the waves, the absurd alternation of day and night, the seasons, even the rocks. I would later learn from Syd that the largest rocks were the youngest, having only recently, in geological terms, solidified from magma when there was still furious volcanic activity in this region. In previous millennia, boulders as large as this one had been gradually pulverized into pebbles and sand that were shuttled out with the tide onto the seabed. The lithosphere is simply an ocean of rocks and sediment. Over enormous spans of time, rocks descend back into the magma. The organic matter by contrast was caught in a madly accelerated series of cycles: the kelp that grows during the summer and fall until it blankets the peninsula's coast, before winter storms uproot its stinking mass onto the beach, a nursery for flies. It was all here, the proof that no alternative to decline was necessary because decline itself is contained within the cycle. Edda's god was the cycle itself.

There were no more meetings that year. Leta and Joanna apologized profusely over email and promised renewed commitment next fall. I didn't bother distributing anything to the group and figured that a clearer path forward, a document that articulated my critique, was necessary before anyone would bother. Syd never wrote to follow up after Pelican Cove, but I ran into him while getting coffee just before Spring Break. He invited me to sit down with him, and his normal cold demeanor was slightly friendlier. He asked for my indication of support on a small-scale internal grant for which he was applying. It was to fund interdisciplinary research, and he was of course putting forward his metabolism project. He needed to show that he had "founded" a research center comprised of at least one department outside his college of sciences.

"Those are the rules of the grant people, not me." He smiled nervously.

"I'm sure."

"Look, I know I could have been in contact with you earlier . . ."

"But it's only now that you need me."

He dropped the smile and said, "You're right, I'm a dick. Look, I'm going to order myself something to eat. Do you want anything?"

He ran off to get in line for food. His phone, which he left on the table, lit up with a text. It was the first time a man other than a family member had ever offered to buy me food. I glanced at his phone just in time to see the name of the sender of the text: Leta. When he sat back down, I didn't see him. I stared at a mirror on the wall opposite us. I saw myself for the first time as someone in public might. A prematurely old-looking woman of average height, a little heavy, with stupid hair and a drunkard's flushed face.

"Fine, I can sign the form." I took a sip of the coffee he brought, and then said, "It was my idea to found the center, you know."

"Of course, thank you. Excellent. I'll send the form to your office this afternoon."

◎ ◎ ◎

It may seem odd that a memoir written by a university professor should continue for so many pages without mentioning classes or students. Let me explain.

By the late twentieth century, the glut in the higher education industry was such that schools competed with one another in a slow-motion agon, with month-long periods of apparent stasis punctuated by stabbing moments of battle. At these moments, usually at the beginning and end of academic terms, sleeping campuses awakened to fight bitterly over star graduate students and faculty. Only there were no outward signs of struggle. Reports would circulate, usually by word of mouth or on social media, that one high-end institution had just lured a rock-star professor from another high-end institution. Or a jubilant young scholar would have her head turned when, beginning around Valentine's Day and culminating in March, she'd received acceptance letters to the doctoral programs from top schools, each flattering her with mention of tuition remission and generous stipends, research opportunities, and travel budgets. She'd post her good news onto her accounts, perhaps, at least initially, intending merely to celebrate. But she'd quickly realize that sharing good news is itself a little form of warfare, against potential competitors as well as any teachers who ever doubted her capabilities. She thus began her own campaign against the young scholars who, with her, would one day apply for the same tiny pool of fellowships and jobs. That was as close as it ever got to bloodshed in academia, with muted, civilized exchanges of congratulations, and silent recriminations and schadenfreude and jealousy.

Together, these schools could be considered a sort of ecosystem. The alpha predators were the lions, the name-brand elite universities such as Harvard, Princeton, and Yale, plus a handful of prestigious schools to the south or west, like the University of Chicago, Stanford, and Duke. The University of X aspired to this category and in internal communications set as its goal the metrics of its closest role model, Stanford. Another variant of predators included falcons like premiere science and technology schools such as MIT and Cal Tech. State systems of publicly funded universities could be regarded as predators, though their budgets were seldom as robust as those of the privates. Of these, the University of California's eight campuses led in terms of reputation and selectivity. The smaller predators, akin perhaps to lone wolves, were the small liberal arts colleges like Williams or Reed, where one could find the same caliber of faculty and students, as well as a greater emphasis on teaching rather than research.

Below this top tier of assassin-like schools was the larger pool of herbivores: state universities, private colleges (secular and religious), and universities. And underneath that bovine layer, a whole landscape of grass and plants: the community colleges. Faculty teaching loads at these humbler institutions were generally heavier, while at the top schools, faculty were generally expected to have "active research profiles." The quality of students was sometimes higher at the top; some students were truly excellent, and many others were just lucky enough to have benefited from the support of family, tutors, and coaches. Despite administrators' claims at leveling the playing field, money generally opened more doors and created more opportunities for networking, enrichment, and broadening of horizons. It was the silent hypocrisy of early-twenty-first-century higher education that as all of us, faculty, students, and administrators alike chased the big money, we pretended to regard education as the tool for correcting social inequalities.

If I sound cynical, it is because I saw the extent to which universities were like the worst of corporate America. They paid sexual predators on staff to leave and disappear quietly, so as to avoid negative publicity. They staged aggressive public relations campaigns to climb in the rankings of the *US News and World Report's* list of top colleges. They yielded to the most craven extremes of political correctness. The contradictions and absurdities of the university system have been documented elsewhere. I write this now as a preamble, for my goal here is to describe what it was to be at the other end of the country, the side opposite the ambition of the Ivy League, the side that boasted of its imagination and forward thinking and proximity to other Pacific Rim countries. The University of X, with its aspirations and hubris, at first seemed the worst place in the world to teach the late Roman Empire, especially as it was experienced in Augustine's North Africa. I had reason early on to be discouraged, for it seemed impossible to convey certain aspects of that existence to young Angelenos. But I gradually began to perceive affinities between Roman Africa and modern California's pretensions at elite education. Both Africa and LA were far away, geographically and culturally, from the center of their respective empires. Africa was solely responsible for Rome's food supply, just as the Central Valley just to the north of Los Angeles fed not only the United States, but much of the rest of the world. At least until the early fifth century AD, Africa was at some remove from the disastrous invasions and civil wars that plagued Rome and Gaul. The West Coast was three time zones away from the nation's capital, and an ocean spanning half the planet separated it from

Asia. Come to think of it, I would eventually joke in my lectures, Los Angeles was the perfect place to teach the Late Empire. But I couldn't push the analogy too far. For while California might in theory have something in common with Africa's physical isolation, California was arrogant in a way that North Africa never was. Most of my students were too young to appreciate this. Just as Augustine wrote of the Romans, those Angelenos were too busy asking the way to the (movie) theater to concern themselves with the barbarians at the gate.

Like many academics, I chose my field after figuring out that school and learning suited me, that I could happily remain a student for the rest of my life. My long-standing love affair has been with late Antiquity, not with students. The passion to teach, so often touted as essential to a good professor, was for me not a passion at all, simply a well-intentioned but detached interest. I have enjoyed teaching, but it would be a lie to say that it was ever my reason for getting up in the morning. I suspect that the same is true for many university faculty, but it would be career suicide to admit as much publicly. So we fabricate teaching philosophies with impossible superlatives. We are all like King Lear's first two daughters, purporting a nearly hysterical concern for our students. On my best teaching days, I had a lot of fun. And I forgot any great class discussion after a day or two. My evaluations said that I was a good teacher, but it would take an idiot not to score well on those sorts of questionnaires. A few students have kept in touch with me over the years. That was how it was, when the administrators' attention was turned, and the true criterion for success remained the amount and quality of academic publications we generated.

During the semester when I visited Pelican Cove with Syd's students, I taught a freshman seminar on the Roman Empire. There is usually one stand-out student in any class, and this time, it was Philip, an enthusiastic, pimply young man who, like most of us, was most interested in the decline, rather than ascent, of the Empire. Philip was delightful thanks to his contributions to discussions. And while I liked him just fine, I was silently horrified at what he represented. In his otherwise ebullient comments during class, he was unable to speak more than three or four words without throwing in the word "like." Southern Californian kids use "like" liberally; I had been no exception when I was young. But Philip's reliance on the word was a tic. Philip spoke openly about his regular use of marijuana, which shocked no one except me, given that recreational use had just been approved in a state-wide proposition. I despaired that Philip was emblematic of his generation. My thoughts no doubt reflected my own aging and increasing close-mindedness. Still, I couldn't shake the sense of my own complicity in the educational failure that produced Philip, through my support for Philip and my aversion to more confrontational teaching methods. Some of my colleagues practiced an "*apprentissage à souffrance*," an education of suffering by means of public and private humiliation of students for mistakes in their classwork. I could have adopted that approach, but I didn't care enough about "educational outcomes" to want to be cruel, to Philip or anyone. I thus wallowed in the vague terrain of the teacher who instructs by example, and who exemplifies mastery of a subject as well as disinterested kindness. In the back of my mind, I knew that my disinterest abetted the mediocrity of my students.

These thoughts troubled me around the time that Philip visited my office hour halfway through the semester. This was itself unusual, as students rarely visited my office hours. I had just distributed a major assignment in the seminar, a paper that asked students to identify "decline" in contemporary American life. Deceptively simple, I argued, because proof of decline is difficult to provide. I assigned them passages from Gibbon and Thucydides, and we discussed the trope of the old embittered observer who complains of the young generation. Philip visited later that afternoon.

"Hey, professor."

"Hi, thanks for stopping by."

"I wanted to ask you about the project." His lips and cheeks twitched with nervousness.

"Of course. Where shall we begin?"

"Well, like, I'm getting hung up on, like, all the times I think about, like, decline without really knowing, like, whether it's real or not."

I will refrain from further use of "like," but Philip's subsequent sentences leaned on the word just as much as the previous.

"Great! Let's start with an example. What about our culture in the past fifty years has declined?"

"Uh, well, I wanted to talk about the music industry, but I don't know if that's okay for this class."

"Sure, it is. Only you'll need to help me out by providing lots of evidence, since I don't know the first thing about it," I chuckled to put him at ease.

"Okay." He seemed satisfied already, but wasn't going to speak further, so I pressed.

"So what has declined in the music industry?"

"Uh, everything! Income for artists, quality of recordings, originality, creativity."

"Is that so? Wow, I must be living under a rock. And how do we define the music industry? Who belongs to it?"

"Well, musicians, obviously."

"All kinds, or just pop?"

"I don't know. Pop and other lucrative genres, I guess?"

"And what do they sell? Surely not music, right?"

He stuttered, "Recordings — at least they used to. But now that recordings are free . . ."

"They are?"

"Yes, through Spotify or YouTube or SoundCloud."

"Okay, so there is still great demand, but the commodity's exchange value has been rendered nil."

"Uh, yeah."

"Do you listen to new music?" I asked, changing angles slightly.

"Yes, all the time."

"And do you like it?"

"Yes, lots of it."

"So why do you say that the quality has gone down?"

He flushed. I was never this Socratic in my classes, and he looked at me with some apprehension.

"I guess it hasn't. There's just so much more of it, so more good music and more bad music."

"Now, this is an industry that earns far less money than it used to, and yet there is more commodity or product than there used to be, a good deal of it of good quality."

"Uh, yeah."

"So what is in decline?"

He didn't know, and I didn't know. We chatted for a few more minutes, but it was clear that he was unsettled. He wrote me that night: "Hey professor—thanks for our talk today, it was informative. I guess I didn't think enough about decline in the music industry. It just seems like the fact that you can't make a living in music anymore shows that it's in decline. But I guess it's more complicated than that. Anyway, here is a song that always makes me think of an old wizard who used to be able to summon dragons. But now, he's dying in his bed. And he turns over and becomes a dragon, and dies." No further explanation, just a see-you-next-week. I listened to the linked song. "No More Sorry," by My Bloody Valentine. It was crystalline and smelled of ash and sulfur. I listened to little else for the next several weeks.

This exchange would have quickly faded from memory, as would have Philip, if it were not for the final project he submitted that semester. There was no trace of his planned essay on the music industry. In fact, there was no essay at all, rather a sketchbook containing twelve pencil drawings and a document entitled "Manifesto." The images were reminiscent of William Blake's art. Fantastical figures — chimeras, angels, impossibly chiseled muscular men — struggling against forces seen and unseen. A blindfolded woman holding a sword aloft, as if in a Soviet propaganda poster. And buildings with hundreds of stories, as seen from the sky looking down. The manifesto was an attempt to adapt Augustine's *City of God* to the present day. Instead of invading barbarian hoards, the enemy was the CORPORATION (all caps intentional), the mega-conglomerate that had destroyed governments, human rights, and ecosystems, even while proclaiming itself the protector of all three.

It was crudely worded, and Philip clearly hadn't read more than the first twenty pages of *City of God*. But it was also brilliant. Every sentence was an admission of the impossibility of further progress. He spared no institution, and offered no blandishment of concern or compassion. A handwritten note at the bottom of the last page thanked me for the class, and asked that I listen to "No More Sorry" while reading his project. "The wizard will return to life if we summon him, and we can, with this song and through hope."

Syd naturally won the interdisciplinary grant. He sent word that summer: "Grant came through. We'll need to meet in the fall. Paperwork and formalities, but maybe also a chance to reboot. Thanks again — S." I lay in bed for the better part of a week after that message, spending hours arguing with him in my mind. My physical ailment worsens with stress, and in my twenties I had become pretty good at managing anxiety, in part through sending myself to Bíldudalur. Now, I was sending myself to dark holes that sapped what little optimism I had cobbled together in the spring. I eventually made a concession to send myself away from the body that was rejecting me a little more each day. After all, it was the body that everyone else saw, that Syd saw, that no one wanted to see. I might as well refuse it too. At the end of the summer, Syd called for a meeting of the Center for Critical Studies of Capitalism, which had somehow accrued a mailing list of around forty members, faculty and graduate students mostly. I wrote to him that it should by rights be I who called meetings for the group. He never responded.

Everything at that meeting unraveled as it had in my visions. Joanna never showed up and sent no explanation. Leta was there, and I was momentarily happy. Then her hand brushed Syd's as she leaned to murmur something. Not a long pause, nothing demonstrative, but everything became clear. Syd excused himself briefly to take a call outside, and I looked at Leta. She smiled nervously and avoided my eyes. When Syd came back in, he began the meeting as if he were a sleazy nightclub host. It looked so easy for him. He had already scheduled two meetings with scholars from nearby institutions, and two other meetings with external funding organizations. He had drafted statements of the Center's goals for those external sources. I objected, "But we haven't even figured out what we are doing."

"True," Syd said, "but this will help expedite that process."

The statements focused exclusively on Syd's research on metabolism and Capitalism. There was nothing on our search for an alternative, nothing on Marx.

I took out the documents I had prepared to present. Philip had, over the summer, expanded his manifesto into a graphic novella. I placed the copy he sent me onto the table. It was strange and repulsive and entrancing, and Syd barely glanced at it, but Leta swooped down on it. After a few moments, she said, "Syd, this is really good. I'm serious."

"We could become like Augustine," I began, but my voice gave out. I wanted to say more — that we could found a new City of God, that we could offer a harbor to those fleeing the oncoming storm of automation, that stasis could be imposed, that no man would ever look at me like Syd was looking at Leta.

"That's great, Annika. Let's include this in the package for the NSF grant I'm preparing. Now, to the matter of a name?" His voice became tinny and lost some of its bite. I sank under the waves. "What's wrong with our name, Syd?" Leta asked. She was looking at me with a frown. "You alright?" she whispered.

"Our name — the CCSC. That's the problem. No one can remember it. It's boring."

"We could take Annika's idea, maybe, and refer to Augustine somehow."

"Nah, then people would think we were Catholics."

I noticed a book peeking out of Leta's bag: the *Edda*. I pointed toward it. She said that she had been reading about Norse eschatology for a new composition. Syd's eyes brightened as she spoke. "Why not the Eddan group?" I was able to spit out.

"'Edda' means 'grandmother,' I think," Leta said.

"Yes."

"Doesn't matter. It sounds good," Syd said, looking at Leta only.

"Why not the Eddan Collective, at least? So it sounds artistic, not just scientific," Leta said, trying to maintain her composure, but Syd's smiling eyes made her crack a smile of her own.

It was done; I slipped under as Syd left. Leta waited for a few moments, trying to be polite, before leaving too. I sent myself to the fjord at Bíldudalur, and was floating near the bottom, laying on my back while staring up at the black night. The moon shimmered in the water.

CHAPTER FOUR
The Malayka[*]

IT IS NEARLY A YEAR SINCE HIS HOLINESS
passed from this broken world to the next, I pray better,
one. I am glad that he did not see what happened to
Hippo, how starvation changed people into demons,
how the abject ate the corpses of their recently deceased
neighbors, how disease laid waste to the town and created little armies of orphans and childless widows and
widowers. His Holiness would no doubt have looked
upon such sorrow with his characteristic serenity, for
he had lived through his own sorrow and knew that
our present life would give us little other than sorrow.

---

[*] Editor's note: This chapter, along with Chapter Ten, are written from the point of view of Possidius, Augustine's close friend
and biographer who was with him at the time of his death. This
chapter would indicate that Possidius made Annika's acquain-
tance, although we have found no outside evidence to corroborate this meeting. These Possidius sections appear in Annika's
handwriting in her journal, and there is nothing to suggest that
she herself did not write them. But they obviously break from
Annika's otherwise first-person memoir, and she never explains
why these sections are included. Nor does she ever mention Possidius in the sections written in her own voice. We are thus at a
loss as to what to make of these two chapters. Because both of
them take place outside of the normal spatio-temporal realm of
Annika's day and circumstances, we might be tempted to dismiss
these as fantasy chapters. Or, we could wonder whether Annika's
ability to send herself away, already at full deployment when she
occupies Syd in Chapter Six, so surpasses her awareness that she
forgets her own identity entirely. Perhaps there is some other
explanation, or perhaps this will remain one of the lingering
questions about the manuscript.

He would have said that this life was a gift, but also a cross; and that we needed to take up that cross with as much humility and love as Our Lord granted us. As a bishop, he could well have detached himself from the suffering of the people, but he instead cried when a father came to him, weeping at his stillborn child. He suffered with us, but he had the wisdom to know that this world's suffering would eventually come to an end.

I am also happy that he did not see the Vandals enter Hippo, bringing with them their Arian heresy. Perhaps Arians are preferable to pagans, and perhaps we should tolerate Geiseric as he tolerates us. At least, that is what some of the townspeople say. But as indulgent as Geiseric has been with the Catholic folk, he has been brutal towards those of us who live in the monastery. I fear that my brothers and I will need to flee soon.

My name is Possidius, and I was blessed to call Augustine my friend. I lived at his monastery in Hippo before founding my own in Calama and returned to Hippo when the Vandals were approaching. I tended to him during his last months and was at his side at the moment of his passing. In fact, I spent most of his last summer by his cot, visiting him daily to pray with him, speak of the old days, and bear agonized witness to the frame that, already gaunt, was losing its remaining weight. I suppose that I could boast of a familiarity with His Holiness that few others alive could have claimed. If my story ended here, I would already count myself the luckiest of brothers for that privilege. Little was I to know that a greater honor was in store. One afternoon in the mottled golden light of his cell, Augustine was sitting up in bed, a great accomplishment. He asked, "Has the *malayka* been here today?"

"I'm sorry, Father?"

"The *malayka*, the one who visits me in the mornings and at night."

"No one has come here, Father, other than I."

He dozed off, and I discounted his words as the momentary emergence of some dream. But the next day, His Holiness in full lucidity apologized for his question and said that he had merely become confused as to the time of the *malayka*'s visit. She liked to come by before dinner, not in the morning.

"Forgive me, Father, I do not know of such things. Perhaps another brother should be called?"

"I do not want to talk to another brother, Possidius."

And, to my profound apprehension, His Holiness began to tell me of the creature who visited him over the past several years. She was, at various moments, a demon, an angel, a spirit, or a *malayka*. She came from another land or another world. She was sinister or holy. She was Augustine's delight and affliction. All of this and more was true, as if there were as many different *malayka*s as Augustine had moods. Needless to say, I was stultified at His Holiness's words, and feared that what he was relating to me in friendship was far better suited to the confessional. But Father's words were measured, and he did not sound as if he were confessing sins of the heart or mind or body. Besides that, His Holiness confessed to me on a daily basis, and clearly was in the habit of divesting himself of the occasional sins that a man of such holiness committed. There was nothing salacious about this *malayka*. I thus feared that His Holiness was experiencing an infirmity of the mind, something that stalked those blessed to live well into old age. Yet again, Father's words allayed my fears. His intellect was as vigorous and discerning as it had been decades before, and I had the word of several church brothers to corroborate my own observations on this point. There emerged but one explanation for His Holiness's stories: he was telling the truth.

But what sort of truth could make such incredible claims was beyond my understanding. The *malayka* first came to Father as he was praying in his cell, composing a sermon. She said that she sought Father's counsel on a matter of gravest importance. And she displayed a keen awareness of His Holiness's life, his writings, and most strangely, the contents of his heart. She knew, for instance, of his thoughts on the Heavenly and Earthly Cities, thoughts that he had not yet refined and condensed into his tome, *De Civitate Dei*, the City of God. Given this impossible knowledge, it is all the more astonishing that the *malayka* would claim to be in such a state of need, for how could any creature who knows the unknowable need anything? But my incredulity aside (Father, forgive me my little faith!), here was her story: she came from a distant land, one whose riches and armies dwarfed those of Rome and Persia and Germania put together. This empire extended beyond frontiers. Although there were many kingdoms with many kings and princes, there was only one empire, and it ruled over every king and every prince as well as every one of their subjects.

The strangest trait of this most dread empire was that it had no emperor. It needed none, for the power that coursed through its veins, by means of commerce and communications and transport, possessed a mysterious ability to seek its own path, through people most disposed to its purposes. That vessel could be a king, but also laborers, slaves, soldiers, even mothers clutching their children. The *malayka* said that a wise man long esteemed for his philosophy had described the "cunning" of this power (the "cunning of reason," she called it), as if the empire itself were alive and supremely intelligent.

Suspending for a moment my dogged skepticism with the *malayka*'s tale, I said that what she thus described sounded like a mighty and thriving land. His Holiness said that he had responded in a similar manner, saying that, provided the empire served and honored and believed in the One True God, His Son Christ, and the

Holy Spirit, this would indeed be an empire for the ages, far exceeding Rome's glory. The *malayka*, however, replied to him that the empire was both godless and pagan. Godless, because most kingdoms within the empire renounced religion of any kind; and pagan, for although the kingdom might have forbidden its ministers to require worship of any deity while fulfilling their duties in government, the kingdom's citizens were free to practice any religion they wished. On that point, the *malayka*'s empire was even more permissive than Rome. *In that case*, His Holiness despaired, *it is an infernal empire, deserving of every calamity God sees fit to bring down upon it.*

Ah, yes, the *malayka* then replied, *now, you begin to perceive the problem. For the empire is both the best and the worst thing ever to befall our world. No force, no kingdom, no legion has ever inflicted greater harm or suffering on mankind, or animals, or plants, or on the land and sea and air. More have been crushed under our empire than have lived or will ever live in your Roman Empire. And yet, my empire has brought a prosperity unimaginable at any other point in history. Never before have so many had enough to eat, safe lodgings, and doctors to treat and prevent injury and illness. It was*, the *malayka* said, to quote another writer from her empire, *the best of times and the worst of times.*

An empire without the One True God is hell-bent on destruction, was all that His Holiness would say in response. And the *malayka* would nod as she patted His Holiness's shoulder, for he had taken to laying his head on her lap as she sat on a stool in his cell. She would pat his head absently as she looked out the little window, tears streaming down her face. I never dared to ask His Holiness about these moments of intimacy, but I am sure as to their chastity. For His Holiness had told me that the *malayka* did not have the form of a woman, but rather a human-sized bird, with feathers that were golden and emerald and beryl. She was the most beautiful creature His Holiness had ever beheld, and in saying this, his voice conveyed not lasciviousness, but rather wonder. She said her name was Annika.

As she comforted him, she asked what was best for the people of her empire. His Holiness never knew what to say to this question, and simply let her talk. *The Church will eventually take the place of your Roman Empire. It will even become your empire! But there is nothing waiting in the wings that will take the place of my empire. Yes,* she would say in response to his questioning eyes, *my empire is in decline. There is nowhere for it to go. There are far too many citizens, and we are running out of fuel. Our success is proving poisonous. But all of this is just in the natural order of things,* she would sob. *What I don't understand is how your god reconciles cycles (for declines of empires are merely part of larger cycles) with redemption? There is no stopping the morbid wheel. It spins and spins. In two centuries, a wise man named Boethius will call it the Wheel of Fortune. Will it ever stop spinning?*

A few of us, she continued, *those who see what is taking place, choose to follow the teachings of a philosopher named Marx who lived over a century before I was born . . . so many centuries after you will have lived. You might think of him as a prophet. He foretold everything that has befallen my empire. And he predicted an uprising of workers, and a transformation of the empire into a . . . better place, a heaven on earth. He was also one who denounced religion and god.* Now it was His Holiness who had tears pouring down his face, despairing at the *malayka*'s godless world. *But, Father,* for that was what she called him, godless though she was, *Father, I have come here and told you of my troubled land because I have hoped that you could offer me advice. Some of us think that the conditions that made our Empire, as well as yours and every other empire, are permanent. If you like, they spring from our original sin, our desire to go against God . . . our desire to steal pears.* Her voice trailed off long enough for her words to make His Holiness grow pale. Her gift permitted her to read words of his that she could not possibly have read. *And others amongst us,* she continued, *those who still dream of another way of being, imagine that we can turn to cycles, to the morbid wheel, for consolation. For perhaps that is what God wants of us after all—to make the cycle of expansion and contraction, of rise and fall, our home rather than an inconvenient stop along the way to our home. Perhaps all our conniving to win, or at least not to lose, is what we must leave behind. Perhaps it is not for us to aspire to Heaven, for that is just another sort of victory, after all. Perhaps the spinning around is holiness already, if we have the grace to accept it as such.*

His Holiness was usually stricken by this point. They always had the same conversation, which always ended in this manner, with the *malayka* solving the very problem she had brought to him to solve. He would always cry with despair, and she would leave him. But, as His Holiness never tired of saying, he savored nothing more in the narrowing horizon of his remaining days than to pray to Our Lord and to hear the mournful voice of the *malayka,* low and soft like the ocean at night.

Two nights ago, as I was lighting my lamp and preparing for a few hours of reading and meditation before retiring to bed, the *malayka* visited me. The word "visit" domesticates it, in fact, for she simply appeared in my apartments, without a sound and with no spectacle. She looked at me patiently as I experienced what to her must have been a ritual of prescribed reactions to her presence: startlement, incredulity, fear. She breathed deeply once my eyes actually stopped their panicked glaring to look at her, really *at her.* "Father Augustine said that you were good at listening." And she patiently heard my demurrals. I claimed inexperience, lack of study, provincial uncouthness. When I had finished, she sighed and said, "I know that you are afraid of me, but I ask you not to mind that fear, Father. If for no other reason than that we share memories of the same good man, I ask that you hear of my symptoms."

"Symptoms?" I was surprised, for His Holiness had never mentioned the health of the *malayka*. And that was how she won me over, through appealing to my curiosity. The *malayka* was born with what her parents were told was a rash that covered most of her body. The midwife tried to comfort them in saying that some of us find this world far more exciting than the womb, and our bodies react with this temporary little tantrum. Only her tantrum persisted. The rash would migrate on a nightly basis, moving between extremities, torso, and face. As she grew old enough to talk, her parents finally learned of other reasons why she was such a fussy baby. Her joints would ache, but not consistently, for she could complain one day of her knees, and the next day, feel well enough to crawl and run like any normal child. The physicians to whom her worried parents brought her could exclude the most frightening scenarios: plague, consumption, palsy. But this left the equally unsettling truth, that there was no word to describe her ailment, that perhaps she, the *malayka*, was the first person to have experienced this illness.

"I didn't realize that *malayka*s could be sick. Or have families."

"I am not a *malayka*," she sighed. "Please, look at my skin." And she held forth her wing, covered with impossibly beautiful feathers of all imaginable colors. In fact, it was only then that I noticed that her feathers changed color subtly, as if their pigments would slowly circulate from extremities to torso to face, in no discernible pattern. I also understood the irreconcilable gulf separating her and our, His Holiness's and my, perceptions of her person. For while she saw human skin afflicted with a rash that, she believed, condemned her to a life of quiet shame, we saw a glorious creature, far too perfect and serene and otherworldly to be human.

"Can you tell me what I have, Possidius?"

"I am not a doctor. Why don't you seek one out?"

"I do not want a doctor. Augustine said that you knew how to listen. You are well read. That should suffice."

My head spun; Augustine must have mentioned that my father was a physician, and perhaps Annika thought that I had learned something of the trade. "I can tell you what it is not," I began tentatively, and then listed afflictions we could rule out.

"I am familiar with this method," she responded. "It is called a diagnosis of negation. It works best when there is some endpoint. When all other possibilities have been discounted, there remains some essential malady which we then dub the condition. This is supposed to provide some comfort to the patient. Only there has never been an endpoint to what ails me, no name to tame it. And because there is no name, I have often wondered whether I am even sick."

I chide myself now for how I responded. For, my father's lessons in my adolescence came back, and I offered a diagnosis. I hastened to assure her that she was indeed sick, very sick. Her breath was foul, and her tongue, otherwise a normal human one even if ensconced in a beak, was purplish and swollen. Her pulse was slippery. She was contending with inflammation, and needed to cool and calm her constitution. Herbs could help, as could diet.

"Then what ails me, Father?"

"A fire, an inflammation that besets your skin and liver and kidneys. You have too much yellow bile. This will kill you, eventually. I just don't know when."

The *malayka* said nothing for a long moment. Her eyes grew soft eventually, and then she said that she was perhaps the most fitting embodiment of what afflicted both our homelands. For our empires were also subject to inflammation that could take the form of civil unrest or war or pollution. Since symptoms change constantly, and because attention spans are brief, no one would think to associate a riot in one part of the world with fires elsewhere, or political gridlock in yet another region. "And how does one cure inflammation?," she continued. "There are no easy solutions, but often the only thing one can do is to will coolness into the afflicted members. When the creams and ointments and herbs are ineffective, there remains the will, which can offer some relief. But the will must embrace the inflammation, must accept that it may always be there, will flare up at times and calm down at other times. It is there, and will respond positively to kindness and mercy. But it will never leave."

I saw from the *malayka*'s eyes that she was drifting, was not even aware of her surroundings. Then she was gone, simply gone, as if she had never been there. I did not see her again for some time.

CHAPTER FIVE
Baptism

AT THE NEXT MEETING OF THE EDDANS, Leta brought a friend, a visiting researcher from Japan named Bam. He was short and squat, with long hair that would fall unkempt in front of his eyes, and he was in a state of perpetual motion and agitation. Bam was an artist who specialized in textiles and handicrafts: crocheting and knitting, macramé, papier mâché. He couldn't remain seated for very long, and ten minutes into the meeting, he was pacing around the table where Syd and Leta and the rest of us were sitting. Bam, I quickly saw, was a consummate reader of texts and images and faces and situations. He feigned ignorance of Syd's poorly contained annoyance with his hyper-activity. But Bam was aware of everything, including Syd's contempt for him.

Bam blurted out that he had never read a word of Marx before a week ago, but that he had read a great deal of Marx over the course of that ensuing week, the entirety of *Grundrisse*. Syd petulantly asked him why he would not have started with *Capital*, for which the *Grundrisse* were just preparatory notebooks. Bam ignored the question, smiling conspiratorially as if we were all in on his prank. "If money circulates commodities, then commodities circulate money," he read from his own notebook, nodding triumphantly at all of us as if it was obvious what he meant. He continued nodding even as an awkward silence settled in, as if we were all sharing his delight with some inaudible music.

"That's intriguing," Syd eventually said, "and now, to get down to matters at hand . . ."

But he didn't finish, for Bam interrupted and somehow succeeded in deflecting the room's attention to me, simply by saying, "We all have Annika to thank for the Eddans being here."

Even Syd was momentarily silent, long enough for me to give the little speech I had prepared but had not believed I'd have the opportunity to give. "As I see it," I began, "there are two paths forward for our group. The first is to conduct research that investigates Syd's hypothesis that the problem of Capitalism — the problem that declining rates of capital necessarily drive acquisitiveness — is in fact inherent to biological processes. Capitalism is natural, in other words. The second path forward is to 'inject' some perspective into our perception of Capitalism. Yes, there are indubitably horrible aspects to Capitalism, but Capitalism is itself only one stage of a much larger cycle. Cycles are inherent to nature. The solution is thus inherent to nature."

I felt Syd's impatience, and I saw skepticism in the eyes of Leta, Joanna, and several of the newcomers. Yet Bam had somehow enthralled all of them into silence. "We are desperately in need of conversion," I continued. "The revolution will not take place by storming the barricades, but through quiet, non-violent conversion — not of others, but of ourselves. This conversion will not be brought about by the sword, but through the heart. So, how do we convert our own hearts? St. Augustine of Hippo, the guy who famously said, 'Make me pure, but not yet,' experienced a moment of profound conversion as he listened to songs sung in church. 'How did I weep, in Thy Hymns and Canticles, touched to the quick by the voices of Thy sweet-attuned Church! The voices flowed into mine ears, and the Truth overflowed, and tears ran down, and happy was I therein.' We who study Roman history know this passage well, but we never stop to consider its ramifications. Sound melted Augustine's heart. How could sound melt our hearts? By extension, how could art save us? I would like to propose that we stage an event at a place called Pelican Cove, in Palos Verdes. Syd invited me on a class field trip there with his students last year, and the sounds there made quite an impression on me . . ."

And I stopped, for Bam's sheltering force field was giving way, and other voices began to drown out my own. Syd cut through the murmuring. "I find it absurd that you would choose to speak of religion and conversion within the context of a Marxist group. Have you even read any Marx?"

Leta hissed, "Syd!," but I responded calmly, "Marx responded to the material conditions of his time and place, where religion was still a matter of obligation and birth. Only the privileged few, like Marx himself, could afford to be atheist and to criticize the institution of religion. We, on the other hand, are free to belong to any religion or no religion. To put it in Freudian terms, we need to internalize the threat of withdrawal of parental love; this produces the superego, the force that can make the children of loving unions into strict disciplinarians, above all with themselves. I am not suggesting that we become strict, only that we fill the spiritual void that neoliberalism necessitates. Others fill that void with fundamentalism, but we choose another path. We choose stasis as form."

Syd made a visible effort to calm himself, and his politician's mask returned. "I don't necessarily agree with your summary of my research. At any rate, for those of you who are newcomers: welcome, and please make yourself at home. Our collective grows stronger with each new member. You'll excuse me if my colleague Annika and I are airing our professional differences in front of you. We both have strong opinions, and Bam is right that it's thanks to Annika that this group got off the ground. But now it's time to get serious. We haven't the luxury to take field trips to commune with nature and listen to sounds."

Some of the group members frowned at him. Sensing that he needed to soften his touch, he continued, "My research is not simply trying to demonstrate that Capitalism is inherent to nature. That is a rather unfair simplification. I'd rather put it as follows: instrumental reason is the will to live. When allowed to function as it wills, life wants to remain living. It will find whatever mechanisms perpetuate its existence. If left to develop sufficiently, it will employ methods to enlist the labor of the poor, on land owned by the rich. This, we of course know, is Capitalism. But like Hegel's cunning reason, the will to live assumes any form it can, in order to persist."

"You know, Syd," Bam began, smiling like a six-year-old boy who was stealing a cookie from the cookie jar, knowing that his mother was watching, "it wouldn't be a bad idea for you and Annika to debate. In public, I mean. Maybe a debate about the cunning of reason. Or just Hegel, in general. While not everyone here might have read Marx," and here he smiled mischievously, "it's clear that everyone here has read Hegel."

"That's not a bad idea, Bam," Leta said. "Good publicity for the Eddans, too." And despite Syd's ill-concealed disdain, I agreed as well, and so it took little effort, from Leta primarily, to convince Syd to plan the first public debate for the Eddan Collective on a weekday evening only two weeks later.

The debate was held in one of the oldest buildings on campus. This wasn't especially meaningful to Europeans with their thousand-year-old universities, or to Americans already familiar with the Ivy League campuses. But the fact that the Webb building recently celebrated its 110th birthday, and that its Reading Room, our venue, was impressively outfitted with reddish oak panels from floor to ceiling, made the faculty somewhat proud. Everything about the room repudiated the architecture and design of the rest of the University of X. Its ten-foot windows were in the original leaded glass (no earthquake-proof, double-paned glass here), and the murals depicted greats from the literary canon from Virgil through Chaucer to Shakespeare. The concerns of building inspectors and critics of canon aside, the room was agreeable even to those of us who had frequented much older and more venerable universities. But there was no one to help with setting up, so Syd and I each positioned our respective podiums, Syd simply carrying his, and me shimmying mine from one corner to the next. Leta and Bam arrived while we were preparing and saw to the microphones and to the screen which carried the single slide, "What Is the Cunning of Reason?" with our names underneath.

Syd and I flipped a coin to determine who would go first; Syd won the toss. He took to the podium, and after a brief introduction, he began:

"Thank you all for coming this evening. I know that I speak for Annika when I say that we are both flattered and honored that you have chosen to spend an evening with us, especially at this busy time of year.

"The format for tonight's debate is somewhat unique. We have a question, as you see: What is the Cunning of Reason? But there are no conventional sides of pro and contra, because Annika's and my positions are not contrary to one another. Indeed, as I expect that you'll see, our positions are in a truly dialectical relationship, which is especially appropriate given the mission of the Center for Critical Studies of Capitalism: to return to Hegel.

"To summarize my position: it is my belief, borne out through empirical data, that the Cunning of Reason for Hegel is what we today would characterize as the will to live. For Hegel formulated his system some

68

five decades before Darwin wrote *Origin of the Species*, and he could not have benefited from Darwin's theory of evolution. That said, it is well-known that Hegel conceived of Reason as a great force, a singular will that uses individuals as it likes, in order to achieve its ends. It would take a philosopher far better equipped than I to unpack everything that Hegel intended here, but suffice to say that Reason and Spirit, at various moments in history, work *through* individuals and their passions, to effect change and growth.

"We cannot deny that humanity is in a death-match with Capitalism. As it is currently being practiced, Capitalism threatens our social relationships, civil governments, democracy, and the environment. All of these points naturally make us ask whether Capitalism is necessarily our fate, or whether we could have chosen otherwise. Better yet, whether we still have the opportunity to choose otherwise. I am currently leading a research team that will show that a capitalist fate is not reserved for humans alone, but can befall other species as well; stay tuned for more on that. My assertion tonight is that Reason's Cunning is using Capitalism, its many failings notwithstanding, to ascend to a higher level in the dialectical cycle. Through Capitalism's ills, humanity will purify itself, increase efficiency in production, and diversify its product base. In sum, Capitalism is the tool by which Reason, as it operates right now, at this moment in history, betters humanity."

That is more or less all from Syd's opening statement; I have reconstructed it from notes I took as the debate was happening, so I may have left out some information. Here was my response:

"I came here today expecting to be more at odds with Syd's argument. But after hearing his opening statement, I predict that my own remarks will strike you as being in what my father would call 'violent agreement' with Syd's position. For, you see, I too subscribe to the concept of the Cunning of Reason. And in agreeing with Syd's description of the Cunning of Reason as the will to live, I adhere to the statement that such a will uses individuals in order to attain its ultimate ends, without necessarily regarding those individuals' passions as good or important. Given this level of agreement, I am left taking issue only with Syd's implicit definitions of nature, and why on earth he could regard nature as wanting or desiring Capitalism.

"For, contrary to anything Syd might claim proves the contrary, there is nothing natural about Capitalism. Expropriation of land and resources does not, in any animal kingdom, lead to or facilitate a market economy. Whatever claims Syd might make (about Capitalism bleeding over into other species) demand a high degree of selective interpretation, a sort of cognitive bias that sees Capitalism wherever it looks.

"Nonetheless, I agree that we should look to nature for help as we explain the Cunning of Reason. The idea of the Cunning of Reason is a term Hegel used in his philosophy of history, but elsewhere in his system, this same concept was called the Doctrine of the Concept. And in still other moments in Hegel's system, he used the word 'teleology' to refer to this same idea.

"Now, the teleology of which Hegel speaks is Aristotle's teleology, the theory that every creature, body part, and organ, all reflect some final end. The teleology of the tongue is to taste; the teleology of the eagle is to fly, capture prey, and reproduce. This theory fell into disrepute when thinkers began to question the intelligence that it assumed lay behind all creation. But Hegel vigorously resurrects it in his *Philosophy of Nature*. Here is what he says:

The teleological standpoint which was formerly so popular, was based, it is true, on a reference to Spirit, but it was confined to external purposiveness only, and took Spirit

*in the sense of finite Spirit caught up in natural ends, but
because the finite ends which natural objects were shown
to subserve were so trivial, teleology has become discredited
as an argument for the wisdom of God.*

"But that is just it. We must see, in all of the chaos of the
present moment, in all the ills of Capitalism, something
wiser than a superficial reading will permit. Something wiser than what is Syd's position, an essentially
Darwin-meets-Nietzsche brand of 'that which does not
kill our species makes us stronger.' Whether we choose
to call this wisdom 'cunning,' or 'teleology,' or even 'God'
is inconsequential. But know that we are looking more
deeply than just for the situational, transient circumstances of Capitalism. We are looking for something more
than just whether Capitalism will ultimately improve
efficiency or the material quality of life for humanity.
We must, therefore, look elsewhere than to Capitalism
for the Cunning of Reason. I will elaborate where to find
such cunning in my subsequent statements."

Only a few moments in my life did I ever feel that
my words and writings and thoughts were received
warmly. For the first few seconds after that opening
statement, I experienced one such moment. Leta was
watching me with her mouth slightly ajar, and she
nodded from time to time. Bam was standing in the
back of the room with his arms crossed and a satisfied
glint in his eyes. Other spectators seemed thoughtful,
but not skeptical. Even Syd looked slightly appreciative,
as if he now had an opponent worthy of his efforts.

But then, things took a strange turn. Before Syd
began his rebuttal—in fact, as he was gathering his
notes and jotting down one last thought before speaking—Bam suddenly shot up his hand and called out,
"May I ask a question?"

Syd answered kindly enough, "We will have a Q&A
after the last speech."

But Bam persisted, which created an awkward ache in the room, for academics were nothing if not cognizant of ritual and protocol. "Syd, before you start, I just want to ask a clarifying question." As he said this, I wondered at Bam's age. His face suggested someone in his late forties, but his mannerisms, from letting his stringy hair fall in front of his eyes, to moving his hands in little undulations, signaled someone much younger, perhaps in high school.

"You seem already to have given up. Do you realize that?" The air turned abruptly from that awkward ache to brittle electricity. People could now hear that Bam was attacking Syd directly. Academics usually clashed over minor differences in details rather than fundamental ideas, which made Bam's frontal assault especially jarring. "You belong to a group that wants to critique Capitalism, right? So where is the critique?"

And after one, perhaps two seconds, the air finally rushed back into the room, and the electricity fizzled into crowd noise. Someone else near the back of the room exclaimed, "Yeah!," as if he had been only barely able to restrain himself from saying as much. I tried to catch Bam's eye, but he didn't look at me for the rest of the evening, as if he were avoiding my gaze on purpose. And, just like that, one exclamation triggered another until the room was loud with conversation, and Syd meanwhile had stepped away from the podium to talk to Leta, who had gotten up from her chair. My brief moment in Hegelian exegesis was over as soon as it began. Because I had already been seated, it was easier for me to remain unnoticed; within a minute after Bam's outburst, the room seemed to have forgotten me, and certainly forgot any mention of Hegel's philosophy of nature. At least that is how I remember it, for I was beginning to slide from my chair to the floor, and Leta told me later that I must have had a syncope, for my tongue went slack and my eyes rolled to the back of my head, and I was voicing indecipherable words. But I remember nothing of my physical comportment, only my growing panic that I was sending myself away without wanting to do so, and I had no inkling as to where I was going. Then my eyes opened, and I was new.

My feet were clad in sandals. I wore beige robes about my body, and a black cloth on my head served as a veil. My body was not my own. I was smaller and shorter, but also younger, and my body did not hurt. I saw a group of similarly veiled women and robed men a few yards away, and an absurd calm propelled me to them. I could still hear Syd's sarcasm ringing in my ears, yet the air was thin and cold and bore the scent of flowers and pine trees. I was hungry and thirsty, and everything was strange and good and right. One of the robed group spoke up, calling us catechumens and saying that baptism would commence in a few moments. We all looked at one another, twenty or so of us, laughing nervously and looking down at the ground. One of the other catechumens was Bam. He was not Japanese like Bam and looked nothing like him, but I knew it was him, for he looked at me with laughing and conspiratorial eyes and nudged me with his elbow.

We started walking toward a building a few hundred yards away. I knew that this was the Basilica that would eventually be named after Ambrose; but that would be much later and after many additions to the edifice. What lay before me now was typical fourth-century Roman architecture, a formidable brick building with a central gable and several arches at ground-level. We were standing in an open-air rectangular court outside the church. And I knew that this was Milan in perhaps 386 or 387, and that I was to be baptized as Augustine watched. We trailed in hesitantly, and the church, small as it was, was packed with standing mass-goers, the requisite witnesses for the ceremony. We slowed our procession as attendees made room for us down the nave, and my eyes took some seconds to adjust to the interior darkness punctuated by beams of sunlight. At the baptismal font stood Ambrose, small and bald and squinting until we were close enough to be recognized. He smiled simply, but not effusively, a humble man with simple but pressing needs: to attract converts, maintain the sovereignty of his church, and spread the Gospel. His eyes met mine briefly, without pause, and that modest smile neither broadened nor diminished. I must have appeared normal to all those around me. We gathered around Ambrose and he began the prayers. We bowed our heads, and then the singing began. It was technically unremarkable singing, at times rather poor. I somehow knew the words and melodies. My eyes drifted to the attendees, and there was Augustine, younger than how I had seen him in my previous visits. He was taller and more vigorous than he was as an old man, but still small, a body totally susceptible to the elements and surroundings. He was standing next to his adolescent son, Adeodatus, the one who would die only a few years later, and whose death would break Augustine's heart and spur him to sell everything and become a priest. Augustine looked at all of us catechumens together, tears streaming down his face. And I then heard what he heard, a chant that repeated a melody no longer than five or six neumes and no wider than a hexachord, and it was the same melody that I had heard the beggar hum in Hippo, the beggar whose mother died in front of me. My heart strained to make sense of this chant, only it could make no sense; for it left an imprint in the mind for only a few seconds until the mind ceased to attend to the bronze sound, like angels' trumpets, and heard it anew. Bam in his tan robes and Roman visage whispered, smiling, "If sounds circulate souls, then souls circulate sounds." And the air was thick with frankincense, and Augustine continued to weep as he held an arm around Adeodatus and Ambrose sang and prayed discretely, the opposite of a modern showman. The singing grew in strength as the laypeople began to join in, our hymn's repetition reassuring them that they too could sing it. The hymn went on for a long time; I do not know how long, only that it had been a bright afternoon when we entered the basilica, and now it was twilight. We filed outside, new converts of Christ, and before Ambrose could begin to congratulate us, Bam said softly, "You know that Syd is as right as you are. Only, think of 'instrumental reason' as 'original sin,' and it will make more sense. We are touched by death from the moment we are born."

We, the newly baptized, stood with a crowd of onlookers, mostly veiled women and children, the families who had prayed earnestly for this day. Bam never left my side, but when the group began to disperse, he turned to face me. The smile was gone from his eyes. "You have been permitted the experience of today so that you would know that you are right. But what you will learn tomorrow will teach you that Syd is right, too." And whereas before Bam had given me the power of speech, he seemed now to have taken speech from me; for while I wanted to ask what he meant, I could form no words with my mouth. He put his arm around me in a friendly embrace as he led me away, but this embrace brooked no challenge. There was no choice but to follow, and following meant walking into blackness.

CHAPTER SIX
Syd

HE AWOKE THE MORNING AFTER THAT
Eddans meeting, disoriented and more tired than usual.
Briefly, he thought that Leta had spent the night, and
he flung his arm around to grasp her in bed. No, he
remembered, she needed to get some work done and
had stayed home. He was sorry she wasn't there. They
had been together for only a few months, but he was
already quietly in love. Most days he felt punch drunk,
never expecting an outcome so simple or sweet.

Today, however, he felt more hungover than drunk.
The messages he read on his phone should have brought
him up to speed. Usually, he was awake after the first
rancorous exchange with a colleague or his chair or,
worse yet, with me. But now, he could not form cohe-
sive thoughts. After a shower and breakfast, he felt
somewhat better, but longed for the coffee he took
weekday mornings at the café across the street from
his office. Until he got that coffee, though, it'd be a slog,
what with missing Leta, trying to feel enthusiastic, and
remembering something that had happened many years
ago when his father took him out to look for rocks.

Syd's father was a mid-level manager in a manu-
facturing firm that specialized in vending machines.
He was also a hobbyist geologist, or "rock hound," as
he called himself. The first time he took Syd out on a
proper rock hunt, Syd must have been seven or eight.
They drove about forty minutes to the outskirts of
Melbourne. There were quarries in this area that were

still operational. Syd's father planned for the trip, giving Syd his own kit with a little hammer, impermeable notebook, and field guide. In retrospect, Syd knew that his father had also planted a piece of linarite in a mound they were searching. For linarite was not native to Australia. This thought made Syd ache, for his father passed away long before Syd deduced the plot. He never had the opportunity to thank him. But on that day, over three decades ago, the discovery of the rock was a miracle for the boy. "It won't always be this way," his father said, holding the object up close. "Most aren't anything near this pretty." But Syd already lost himself in thought: *There are windows in churches far away that give off this light, a blue that deepens from glacial to oceanic.* But there were no walls to encase this light, so the blue fell off into black or purple. The rock was small, just the size of Syd's fist. He swooned in its depths, and shook his head to free his gaze.

Syd reveled in the memory of a moment he hadn't considered for many years. Could his father have known what the linarite would do to him, how that first glimpse of impossible blue wounded him? Someone, perhaps a philosophy professor, had later told him of something St. Augustine had said, that the five senses were wounds, and that while the desert fathers like St. Anthony tried to cauterize their wounds through solitude and abstinence, Augustine preferred the treatment afforded by the Liberal Arts, which soothed the wounds of the senses like a balm. Small as he was, Syd at that moment learned that beauty can inflict hurt even as it delights the eye. With the benefit of hindsight, Syd now felt that all his subsequent studies and works were attempts to assuage that first injury. Intellectual contemplation palliated the pain, a little, anyway. But it also ensured that the offending object—the linarite and other beautiful stones, and as Syd would discover later, novels and poetry and music—would remain active in his system, secreting their poison in doses too small to notice.

I learned two things in that first half-hour of being inside Syd. He already knew of Augustine. And he had a beautiful voice. Until the moment when he ordered his coffee at the counter, I had never realized what a lovely voice he had.

◎ ◎ ◎

The coffee didn't help. Syd walked slowly back home, feeling worse than he ever remembered feeling, yet with no obvious symptoms beyond fatigue. If this is what true depression feels like, Syd thought, then he'd take back every skeptical thought he'd ever entertained about those who described depression as debilitating. There was a slowness in his movements, a heaviness that dragged thoughts back down into the recesses from which they briefly emerged. It was as if he were full, but not pleasantly, just preoccupied.

He lay down on his bed and stared up at the ceiling, expecting to fall asleep, but sleep refused him. He'd think about the Eddans, he resolved—that was sure to bore him into unconsciousness. *That twat Annika was always going on about the books she read. Especially Augustine and Hegel. As if she were the first person ever to read Hegel, like she's something special.*

Even though he should have moved on in his thoughts to ponder something else, Syd lingered and spun with thoughts of my stupidity.

Hegel wasn't perfect. He wondered if Annika had read Hegel's *Philosophy of Nature*. Of course, it was wonderful—Syd would never say so in front of Annika, but he loved Hegel deeply—but it was premised on an error so fundamental that Syd regarded all of Hegel, indeed, all of the philosophical project in the West—as a beautiful failure. Hegel felt that humanity was the summit of the animal kingdom; fair enough, many others thought the same, and who was Syd to go against the grain? But the dialectic, having traversed mechanics, physics, and finally organics, would then leave nature altogether in order to become Spirit. Life achieves its potential when it dissolves the divisions between self-consciousness. Fine, but then why would Hegel move so quickly onto Spirit, when as Hegel himself said, Earth was the greatest organism? Could he not have seen that Earth contained all that there was to know about Spirit and life and grace?

He was decidedly not feeling himself today. The thoughts he was indulging were beneath him, like how he was when he was a teenager. Hegel was an amateur geologist of sorts, a studier of gems. He perhaps knew of linarite. He almost certainly knew of the stabbing sustained by the heart, when for the first time one gazes on a color the mind has never imagined. We are blasé about color today, what with textile dyeing and Photoshop and instant access to any image from any location. Despite all of that convenience, it still pained Syd to see a precious stone. How much more, then, must it have wounded Hegel to see something like linarite? Syd wished he could have asked Hegel. But he already knew something of his answer; for Syd knew something of Hegel's Doctrine of the Concept, having read of it for the first time many years ago. His mates said he was pretentious for reading, or as they said, pretending to read the *Science of Logic*. He retained little from the first time around, but there was still his recurrent thought that Hegel had succeeded in putting into formal prose the feeling that Syd had upon waking too early every morning. He had withstood that feeling in multiple permutations to the point that he could barely artic-ulate the experience, but one in particular summed it up: bleary-eyed, sitting on the toilet in the dark at half past three, staring at an old squash ball that his father had decreed was to become a cat toy. The cat never once tried to play with it. Syd stared at the object, and felt the presence of the other objects around him: the hand towel, the bar of soap, the soap dish, the toilet paper, the toothbrush and toothpaste. He then knew, *knew* with unsentimental conviction, that the only thing that separated him from any of these objects was his silly sense of self. Only, at that same moment, he imagined a third-party observer—an archangel, perhaps—watching him and the hand towel and the soap bar and dish and toilet paper and the squash ball. To that archangel, Syd and everything around Syd possessed an equal objectivity, and an awareness of that objectivity. Syd knew that he was playing fast and loose, that trained philosophers didn't talk this way, that he was likely wrong. But he remained certain that what the archangel perceived in him and all around him was Hegel's Concept, that it permeated all objects, ideas, affects, and possibilities, and was now to be his code word for "God" for as long as he needed a code word for such things.

Only, Syd lacked any illusions as to the nature of the Concept. It was not a benevolent force that wanted the best for us or animals or plants or rocks or Earth. Just as the archangel who gazed upon Syd that morning so many years ago was not a warm and loving presence, although it was not malefic either. Indeed, Syd had forgotten all about the idea of an archangel watching him until now, for now, too, he felt observed by a third party, a neutral witness. A *malayka*, he thought. Only that word meant nothing to him. It was as if it appeared for his mind's eye to read, and it felt right and appropriate to this context. Yet, try as he might, he could remember no meaning, nor ever seeing or hearing it before.

Syd's mother was French. She was loving and kind to Syd and his father, but seemed inconsolable that her student romance with the Australian she had met at a university in California had led to motherhood and marriage and a life on the bottom of the world, far from her language and everyone and everything she held dear. She spoke to Syd exclusively in French, so Syd was fluent in French, although he had few occasions to be so at his current job. His mother had also bequeathed to him a refined taste for books and music, for she herself had been a punk before responsibility had cowed her into small-scale, perpetual panic. He felt far too weak to roll out of bed and play some music on the stereo, so he settled for remembering music in his head. First, Stereolab's "Crest": his mother played it for him for the first time when he was young, even younger than when he found the linarite. There his mother was, dancing awkwardly and singing, her French-English accent perfectly imitating Laetitia Sadier's French-English accent, for the two were both French expats who moved to Anglophone lands for love; they both had short, asymmetric haircuts, and both were convinced that Capitalism was falling apart at the seams, and that a better world was possible once class divisions and war and religion were all eradicated. She traced tapestries with her fingers that mirrored the comforting organ drone of the song. Syd eventually got up and began laughing and stomping along with her, as they both chanted in their French-English accents: "If-there's-been-a-way-to-build-it-there'll-be-a-way-to-des-troy-it-things-are-not-all-that-out-of-con-trol." Syd's father looked on good-naturedly from his desk in the corner of the living room, not really disapproving so much as bemused. "You don't think that's a bit heavy for him, Cécile?" he asked. *"Mais c'est beau, et c'est la vérité,"* his mother responded, smiling as she caught her breath once their dervish had spun itself out.

It was one of the few memories Syd had of his mother smiling, for not long after that, Cécile's mother had a stroke, and Cécile could not afford the time off from work and domestic duties to fly to Paris immediately, but she resolved to go in January when Syd could spend summer holiday with his father and aunts. Cécile would then relieve her sister, who had their mother move out to rural Auvergne to live with her. A week before Cécile was to leave, her sister was killed in a car accident, only Cécile learned of it five days after the fact, and a day before her planned departure. Their mother sat alone in Cécile's sister's house, unaware from the stroke but still subject to pain and hunger and discomfort. Because Cécile's sister lived far away from even the closest neighbor, no one heard their mother's cries, first panicked and loud and then diminishing in strength, until she too passed away, soiled and dehydrated and confused. Cécile discovered all of this when she prevailed upon the local police station to send someone to check on her sister's residence. She took the flight for which she was originally booked, for now it was too late to drop everything and fly home in a panic. Cécile returned to Australia a month later, looking a year older and with movements in perpetual slow motion. Her subsequent existence was equal parts guilt and anxiety for Syd and his father, the two people left to her in the world. The deaths of her sister and mother were her fault, she knew, not that God punished her, for she believed in no god. And she would walk a tightrope from now on, for the sake of Syd and his father. Disaster had befallen her once, and could come again at any time.

Syd loved his mother, and the two had a harmonious relationship. Yet he had no patience for her fear of disaster. He marveled that what he felt towards anyone who worried or predicted a bad outcome was callous disregard. He should have acquired the ability to commiserate. And he could, at least with people while they were actually experiencing hardships. But impending disaster had, for Syd, taken on unbreakable associations with his mother: the paralysis of doubt, vagueness, and emotional inaccessibility. Disaster was bad enough. But living a life ruled by the threat of disaster was a sure way to dispense with lightness. Syd sought lightness, paradoxically, in the Earth. He chose geology because he loved the integrity and consistency of the links between microscopic and macroscopic. He learned to explain exactly what in its molecular structure gave a rock or crystal its specific qualities. What he saw was what he got. And he loved the look of all rocks, not only the stunners like linarite. He loved biting them gently to test their hardness; he loved holding them up to the light. Syd took the requisite courses in college on biology, and had a healthy appreciation for life science. But he never understood why biology majors never shared his enthusiasm for the classification of minerals. There was enough diversity in the stuff of the Earth to study over several lifetimes.

At this moment, Syd was lying on his right side, somewhere between fetal position and flat on his stomach. His hips and lower back ached, and he was sweating profusely. He hadn't been truly ill in years, and so was resigned to the idea that he was due for the flu. He stared at the alarm clock's red digital numbers: 9:48 am. That red, he just then noticed, was comprised of many tiny dots of red light. Were they pixels? Did pixels even exist in the LED era? That red...it should have been better. More realistic, more like any of the reds he had seen in rocks and gems. You'd think they'd be able to nail a primary color. But no. Somehow this digital red was wrong, mendacious, thanks to its uniformity. It left temporary scars on his retinas. It bore no relationship to any red found in nature. Then Syd understood, for that red was the red of the tail of the dragon that had curled itself into a ball at the foot of his bed. The dragon appeared to be sleeping. Its chest rose slowly, and each exhalation produced something between snoring and the sound of a dulcimer. Syd didn't know how long it had been there, nor how long he had been ignorant of its presence. He thought to jump out of bed, but now his body was nearly completely immobile, and all he could do was turn away from the dragon and back to those red digital numbers. His mouth lay open in horror; he began to drool on the pillow. And so, until 11:43 am, he lay in a paroxysm of terror, praying that the dragon would disappear or stay asleep forever, at least long enough for Syd to regain control of his limbs.

But the dragon awakened at 11:43 am, lifting its long neck and swerving to gaze at Syd. It did not seem concerned or surprised at Syd or its surroundings. It behaved as if it were at home. But it looked askance at Syd once it realized that Syd was looking at it, saw it. It blinked its golden eyes, whose pupils were circular and not feline slits as Syd might have expected, and spoke with no particular hurry: "You're finally awake."

It was all Syd could do to respond, "I wasn't asleep."

"You have been asleep for your whole life," the dragon said, after yawning. The metallic strumming Syd first heard when the dragon appeared was still present, louder when the dragon spoke, but present even when it inhaled. It sounded as if the dragon had iron billows inside it, or a dozen light hammers that struck steel strings like raindrops.

"And yet you are now awake," the dragon continued, now scrutinizing Syd. After a few more yawns and some stretching, it said, "You are in danger, you know." It stared portentously at Syd, evidently waiting for a reaction that did not come. Slowly, for his jaw was stiff, and his tongue and cheeks numb, Syd said, "People have been telling me that my whole life. We are all in grave danger, all the time." He sounded drunk, but his thoughts were clear enough.

The dragon frowned. If such a thing were possible, it looked revolted. "You squander this opportunity to see clearly!" it hissed. Syd, in turn, grew furious at the impertinence of the dragon, who was just like all the other doomsayers who made life unlivable. He was furious, too, with what these prophets of catastrophe had done to his mother, who feared more than she loved.

The dragon was impressed, despite itself. It was accustomed to human terror, bargaining, even admiration. It had never before encountered fury. "Get out of here," Syd whispered.

"Your time is over. Prepare yourself for the recriminations that will come."

Syd mouthed, "Leave me alone," before falling into the sleep that had evaded him all morning.

But the dragon was there even as he slept, purring its dulcimer sounds in, then out. The dragon was reclined next to a stream in the middle of a forest clearing. It was addressing a woman-bird—that was the only way Syd could make sense of the creature—who stood perched on a branch three meters or so above ground. She looked down at the dragon, her two arms outstretched, only the arms were not arms, but wings. Syd thought that he should be disgusted with this monster, but instead, he felt the same sinking he first encountered with the linarite. *My god, she is beautiful.* Her entire body was covered with feathers that were generally iridescent, although one color might take up a limb or patch of the torso, and slowly flow elsewhere on the body. Now, dark transparent blue predominated, the color of linarite, and her wings were amber. Neither the dragon nor the woman-bird seemed aware of Syd's presence.

"You never cease to amaze me," the dragon said, "my transcendent *malayka*." There was that word again.

"Don't change the subject. What will he do?"

"What he is meant to do; what he will have no choice but to do."

"You're a cop-out."

"Yes, so you've told me." The dragon looked off at the stream, making no attempt to hide its aggravation.

"You'd prefer for him to accept blame for something of which he is innocent, than to admit that life is chaos. There is little culpability among them, only among outliers who should indeed be punished. The majority of them do what they should do, what they are educated to do. They may not be angels, but they are not demons either. They are, each of them, little shards of chaos that reflect the chaos of the universe Our Father created. They can't be blamed for that chaos."

"You always talk in badly written prose. Did you know this about yourself?"

"Stop changing the subject."

"Oh, don't worry, I'm not changing the subject. I have plenty to say about the subject at hand."

"Well, go on then." All this time, the *malayka* was motionless, wings spread and head lifted, as if the beak that pointed slightly upwards were some indicator of satisfaction. Syd caught himself thinking that he'd love to knock this miraculously beautiful creature off her perch, and make her smell the earth, and beat out of her this self-satisfied shanti-om cosmic hippie shit that he often saw, especially among the female academics he knew.

The dragon, meanwhile, had its own spleen to vent. "They don't think in those terms. Justice is very important to them. It reassures them to think in terms of responsibility. Chaos is too horrible; for them, it points towards God's absence, not presence. Ah, but I see that you've infected me, and it's now I who am speaking badly written TV script. No matter—he will come to accept the guilt that will be attributed to him. He will plead guilty. The phenomenon of false confessions is very interesting—do you know of it? Sometimes, they feel that it's easier to accept blame, for someone must accept blame if their notion of order is to remain intact."

Syd continued to watch their conversation, which deteriorated into meaningless statements about falling, digging, the smell of dirt and moss — things he couldn't decipher and had no desire to decipher. He wanted to leave, to walk in the forest, which looked inviting and miraculous and calm. And the stream looked delicious, too, and Syd then felt that he had never been as thirsty as he was then. But, no, the dream didn't let Syd choose where to go. He simply walked to the dragon, who didn't look at him but nonetheless seemed unsurprised at Syd's being there. Syd straddled the dragon's back and held two dorsal scales with his hands; and, without a word, the dragon rolled into its side and then sunk into the earth, with Syd clinging to his back. They dove into the ground as if it were water, and a brittle despair welled up in Syd as he saw the underbelly of that which he was supposed to love, that to which he had dedicated his life, now dark and putrid and cold where it should have been warm and glittering and strong.

He slowly awoke, having lost any sensation in his pinkies. It happened sometimes when he slept, and he used to wonder if it indicated a serious problem. But now he knew better, and said to himself that his only problem was that he had had such a stupid prophetic dream. *For of course this dream portends something, something that I will understand later today or this week or next year. Why did it have to be such an embarrassing dream?* What he really needed was to see Leta, see her undress and crawl into bed and kiss him. If he could see all that, perhaps, he'd exorcise these stupid, precious dreams. But it was all Syd could do to sit up, and even as he wiggled his pinkies, his head was faint, and spots floated in his vision. Leta had not responded to his messages from the morning, and again, was not answering her phone. He'd have to content himself with remembering their time together, undressing and kissing and climbing into bed. This would have to do.

Syd had noticed Leta immediately, at that first meeting with Annika. He had begun to despair at first, seeing Annika and Joanna. And then there was Leta, her black hair long and cascading down her shoulders, dressed in a black turtleneck, black miniskirt, black stockings, and black cross-laced boots. He had made fun of artists who wore only black, but none of them looked like Leta did. He suffered through Annika's speeches and interminable emails, but no further meetings had been planned, so Syd emailed Leta to propose talking more about intersections between geology and art. *Good grief,* he had thought, *I might just as well ask to show her my etchings.*

But she wrote back to say 'yes,' and the coffee date lasted two hours and then migrated down a block to a pub, where it lasted for another two hours. Syd was assiduously unflirtatious. They could sit there all night as far as he was concerned, and talk about post-capitalist utopias or climate change, or read the phone book—it didn't matter, as long as he got to look at her beautiful face and hear her bell-like voice. But Leta more than made up for Syd's passivity, first touching him lightly as she told a joke, in anticipation of the punchline. Then, softly squeezing his hand as she sighed, saying what a relief it was to find someone here with a sense of humor. She blushed, she sighed, she laughed, each time finding some new way of grazing his shoulder or hand. Closing time came, and he offered to call her a taxi, and she said he'd better make it for two, that she had some fantastic weed at her place, and that she wanted very much for him to spend the night.

"You know that we're breaking the rules," he said as he began to caress her cheek and neck in the cab.

"You're not my supervisor, and this is no hostile work environment," she murmured, and they stumbled out of the car and to her door, and made love first before smoking the weed. He looked at her afterward, impossibly beautiful as she stared up at the ceiling, naked and blowing smoke and tracing its contrails with her painted nails. How had he gotten to this point, with this woman, after years of ogling women online, women with no past or future, who sold their bodies out of necessity? Syd knew his worth and could rate himself dispassionately. He was in decent shape because he ran and biked often. He was of average height. His face was passable; he didn't stick out from being either handsome or ugly. Entirely average and unremarkable. And women had choices, and careers, and so his prospects as the leading academic geologist of his generation, however impressive in a tenure dossier, would guarantee him nothing in the way of a soul mate. Besides, he had companionship from a few casual friends, and the work was always interesting, always new. With no serious ambition for romance, and absolutely no interest in marriage or children, Syd was left with no way to interact with attractive women other than through pornography. And while he loved and respected his mother, following the example of his father, Syd never tried to seek out a living, three-dimensional female, when all of his immediate needs were satisfied in the safest anonymity.

So here he was now, in bed with an artist-sylph who read philosophy and created sound installations, who wore her hair up in a gently chaotic tangle of black strands, who smoked weed after she made love, and who somehow chose him as her lover, at least for one night. Syd was certain that it would not happen again, so he dispensed with sentimental pillow talk.

"Can I tell you now," he chuckled as she bit his ear, "now—ouch, that hurts—what I'm really working on?"

"Please," Leta murmured.

"Marx was always sympathetic to biology. Did you know that?"

"Well, you mentioned his biological metaphors, but I'm not sure that that counts as sympathy."

"Yeah, but it's more than that. He was a fan of Darwin, a great fan of *Origin of the Species*. He thought that there was continuity between his own work and Darwin's theorization of survival of the fittest."

Leta waited for a moment, and then said, "And you're setting about to prove that continuity."

The pot was hitting him hard, and he watched himself become unnecessarily insistent, unnecessarily because Leta was watching his every word, every gesture, with drugged adoration. "I'm going farther. I've been running tests on basic metabolic processes. Marx, apparently independently of all science, deduced the theory of the declining rate of profit. And science, meanwhile, came up with things like the concept of friction, which explains why the inertial tendency for a body in motion to remain in motion doesn't work on Earth. And Marx's theorem, M-C-M — there has to be a mark-up, because there is always energy lost. The three laws of thermodynamics: you can't win, you can't break even, and things are getting worse all the time."

"I don't think I understand what you're talking about," Leta drawled.

Syd went on, "I'm also reading a lot of evolutionary biology." He mopped his brow. "Did you know that eukaryotes — what we would consider to be the first proper cells, with cellular walls and nuclei and Golgi apparatuses and cytoplasm — they came along as a result of strands of RNA invading an archaeon? Soon, well, relatively soon after that, division of labor began."

"Do tell," Leta smiled, but she was getting drowsy too, and curled up into a ball stuck up against Syd.

"Organs became charged with specific duties. And, all the while, the invaders, the foreign RNA, directed all these processes. They expropriated the workers."

"Hmm," Leta mumbled, almost asleep.

Syd gazed on her naked shoulder and back, chalk-white in the moonlight, and whispered, "There is no justice, because everything that makes us up is predicated on theft and slavery." *Everything, Syd thought, except you, who somehow thought to give me this gift of your body, your breath, your embraces. You will give them to someone else tomorrow or next week or next year, and I don't mind. For one night, I was the beneficiary of grace.*

And yet, that grace stayed on, and even blossomed. He called her his Jane Birkin, for he loved it when she wore her hair down and unattached, hanging straight as she walked with her tailored coat and boots and melancholy eyes. "And I'm ugly like Serge," he said.

"No, Serge was very handsome, it's just anti-Semites who said that he was ugly."

"Well, if a Ukrainian-Jew frog with big ears could charm Jane Birkin, I guess it's possible that an Aussie frog like me could woo you, my beauty."

He didn't speak to her much about his Marxism work. That first night when he'd mentioned it, she'd fallen asleep, and had never asked about it afterward. But she asked him often enough about the day job, predicting earthquakes.

"It will come. The Japanese have already a workable set-up, we just want to extend the advance warning time from seconds to hours, perhaps even days." They were slurping noodles at an udon shop in the South Bay; it was their plan to try as many different Japanese restaurants as they could.

"This will change things," Leta said.

"You bet. Insurance companies are going to hate us."

"Yeah, because they depend on acts of God."

"Yep."

Leta thought for a moment, then said, "You're effectively destroying the very category of 'acts of God.'"

"Was there ever such a thing?"

"Of course not, but it was a thought-fiction to explain phenomena too complicated to describe causally."

"Been reading Joanna, have you?"

91

"No," Leta laughed. "But we collectively used to blame God, or providence, or fate for earthquakes. And even when we understood seismic processes, their unpredictability helped maintain the illusion that they were arbitrary—at the discretion of impenetrable forces. If you make earthquakes entirely foreseeable, you remove any question of guilt or responsibility."

"You are so lovely when you eat udon and discuss ethics."

She smiled, and leadingly said, "But . . ."

"But . . . I'm not sure how guilt ever entered into the discourse surrounding earthquakes."

And Syd continued not to understand as Leta went on, but it stuck with him into the evening. The mystery of disaster, the fact that it could not be foreseen, made recriminations irresistible. Insurance companies could charge their premiums as a way of managing risk, of imparting to clients some responsibility for their choices. Syd's mother blamed herself for her sister's and mother's deaths, knowing full well that she was in no way guilty of wanting their deaths. It was rather that the choice to live in earthquake-prone areas, or to leave one's mother to the care of a reclusive sibling, was the damning choice, because any such choice entailed a surrender to inscrutable forces that could turn malefic at any moment. If Syd's project were successful, it would be akin to the polio vaccine, of turning an unknowable act of God into something as banal as scheduling a fire alarm inspection. This was not to say that damage could be entirely headed off. But just think: if the Sendai earthquake had been predicted perhaps a week in advance, the workers might have been able to prevent the meltdown at the nuclear plant, and the fishermen could have been warned not to take out their boats. And, when Syd was a child, if someone had invented a contraption that warned of imminent disaster, Céline could have flown back home a few days before her sister's accident, and they would have together taken care of their mother, perhaps by finding her an assisted living facility, a nice one, so that she'd live out her days in comfort and company. And Syd would have had a mother, an attentive mother who was not unreachable in her guilt, someone who laughed and sang and danced like she did when he was little, when they sang, "If there's been a way to build it, there'll be a way to destroy it, things are not that much out of control."

Syd was always good at drawing, and during his fourteenth summer, when his voice took less than one week to break from pre-adolescent squeaking to more or less its current baritone, he learned how to put those artistic skills to good use. He had always been partial to women's bodies, but his own recent physiological changes heightened his awareness of female pubescence. He approached these metamorphoses with clinical precision. He'd spend the better part of the afternoon sketching girls' chests, neighborhood girls whom he knew since kindergarten, girls who still annoyed him or, at best, with whom he was distantly friendly, but certainly not in love or even in lust. He was still only fourteen, after all, and while he didn't want to have sex with these newly unfamiliar bodies, he did want to stare at them, and consider the implications of breasts, armpit hair, hips, and the mercenary ease with which these girls inhabited these new bodies. They were expertly aware of the enthrallment of boys around them. Some girls were mean about it, but others were gentle and sensitive, somehow already possessing a respectful gravity about the business, knowing that previously sensible boys were now reduced to base liquids, and not wanting to rub their noses in it.

Syd sketched them, these neighborhood girls of summer, as an art student might. He made studies of one girl's chest, five pages of bikini tops. For another, he focused on her swelling hips in boyshorts—eight iterations' worth. For Christy, the closest thing in his life to a crush, he drew the lips, a mouth that, always pretty, was now arcane and powerful, something that, on another girl, would have frowned cruelly, but that on Christy was merciful, and all the more beautiful for it. Syd was a capable draftsman, good enough to render salient traits in an identifiable manner. So when one of Syd's mates took off with his sketchbook while Syd took a break from drawing to jump in the pool, it didn't take long for every kid in the subdivision to discover with horrified pleasure that Syd was obsessing over Kirsten's breasts and Amy's bum, and above all, Christy's mouth. By nightfall, the verdict was conclusive: Syd was guilty of being a raving pervert. If he foamed at the mouth while exposing himself in a stained raincoat, he would not have seemed guiltier. By bedtime, parents called Syd's parents, more concerned than incensed, delicately asking if Syd had long had these unhealthy fixations, and had they considered therapy? That was it, as far as Syd's high school social life was concerned. From then on, he was his year's student-most-likely-to-become-a-registered-sex-offender; and while the first few months of opprobrium were hard to bear, Syd eventually grew resigned to the role. He did, after all, love women's bodies; it was just a question of being discrete.

The slate was cleaned somewhat when he went off to university. But by then, his habit of hanging back was ingrained. He never initiated conversations with women, except in class or professional settings, and he treated them with detached respect. At parties, he was the one among his mates who presided above the action, a supercilious air to him. Occasionally, a woman would try to flirt with him, and then give up, believing that she wasn't pretty or interesting enough. In truth, Syd was simply managing his risks, and while the episode in his adolescence was unfortunate, it was something from which he walked away unscathed. Stakes were higher now, and he'd never again risk the damage of an accusation.

You'd never be able to sense any of this by looking at him. Syd had abandoned his khakis and schoolboy haircut. He went shopping in secondhand stores, looking for anything that suggested cool, heterosexual profligacy. He wore aviator sunglasses as a matter of course, even indoors as long as he could get away with it. And that part of him that he used to keep in check, his Francophone side, he began to cultivate, through listening to what he called *sleazy French songs*. The instigation for this was as follows: the only time before Leta that he had slept with a woman was when he was twenty, and it was both the most wonderful and terrifying experience of his young life. The Earth moved, the angels wept, and all that, but he was very drunk when it happened, and not sure that Sadie wasn't also. Consent needing to be given rather than assumed, he asked himself right afterward whether what happened could be called rape. But Sadie got up from the bed naked, and smiling, started a record on the turntable: Serge Gainsbourg's *"Je t'aime moi non plus."* It was Syd's first taste of post-coital music, and as Jane Birkin's breathy, accented French got closer to climax, Syd grew calmer. Sadie was clearly harboring no second thoughts or regrets, having nestled happily into the crook of Syd's shoulder, laughing and sighing.

Long after Sadie faded from view to become just a happy, sweet memory (for they couldn't last, not a couple called Sadie and Syd), what remained in Syd was that association between Gainsbourg's cool and Syd's innocence. Gainsbourg might have known how to sing well, but in *"Je t'aime . . . ,"* he bedded the girl by hanging back, by talking with a bedroom voice, by hiding whatever great love he might have felt, and saying merely "me neither" every time Jane opened her heart to him. If this is what it took to have the sort of romance he silently wanted, an affair with a bohemian nymph; if pretending to be a lecher was what it took, then he'd dress the part. Syd began to listen to as much French pop as he could get his hands on, and while little of it could match the perfect deliberate casualness of "*Je t'aime moi non plus*," much of it shared with Gainsbourg a quality that he found difficult to articulate. This quality was not housed in lyrics, for it appeared in songs with lyrical themes that ranged from sex and love and politics to Paris to dying in battle. No, Syd mused as he lay in bed one night, pleasantly tired after watching some women online and listening to some sleazy pop, the sleaze that Gainsbourg and this whole lot trafficked was all about giving in to low expectations. It was within their grasp to avoid being louche, to evade musical clichés, to find a means of musical expression that didn't sound embarrassing. But they chose sleaziness instead, because after everything is said and done, folks more readily believe a false confession than a truthful declaration of innocence.

This night was to repeat itself innumerable times. He'd spend only enough time on some smut site to satisfy himself. His tastes were relatively simple and, he thought ruefully, probably reeked of bourgeois-light sexism — no kink or fetishes or violence, just straight-ahead, good old fashioned chauvinistic objectification. After it was over, he'd abruptly put on some melancholic French pop, maybe Dutronc or Tellier or Air, and he'd read the latest research on seismic prediction, or when he really wanted to treat himself, trawl amateur rock hound sites for the latest in exotic rock and mineral finds. And he'd think that these singers were perhaps just like him, tired of the theatrics of proclaiming the correct politics and feminist allegiances. Their music, with its questionable synthesizers and vocoders and auto-tuned voices, gave into the lie that was told about them and all men of their type, those white straight men who were as horrified as anyone with the abuses of their fathers' generation, and who knew that their statistical advantage in the workplace and in life was due in some part to those abuses. And he would usually end up looking for linarite discoveries, and in contemplating the impossible blue of random samples from Chile and Mongolia, he'd wonder if Tellier and Air and maybe even Gainsbourg kept their best music at home, locked up, only for their wives to hear. And maybe those wives, Amandine and Jane and whoever else dared to give her heart to a French roué, would be the only ones to know of their husbands' innocence, and why they confessed to crimes they had never committed. It was easier, Syd would think before nodding off, since the end was coming anyway.

Syd studied risk management at school even as he managed his own risk. Obscure forces that lived far below the earth's crust, the bed of all that was fine and noble in Syd's cosmology, disrupted everything above: rocks, sediment, the oceans and continents and all the life they bore, all believing that there was such a thing as stability. But that was just it, he began to realize while yawning through his one required biology class at university. Only humans, with their notions of guilt and innocence, cherish anything so preposterous as a belief in stability. Life knows better, even its most rudimentary forms. The green and grey mold cultures he grew in lab class, those that reeked more with each passing day as they overtook the pink agar bed of the Petri dish, knew the truth and abided by it with no twinge of conscience. However well it had grown, mold wanted to grow more. It had to expand, completely and filthily, until it overtook every millimeter of free space in the dish; and after that, it would grow up the sides of the dish and onto the lid, polluting itself with its excrescence until it either ran out of shit to eat or else poisoned itself.

But this was his second year at university, the year when he'd take his labs in the morning and then run to his economics class in the afternoon. His professor wanted him to read the standard bibliography of Capitalism and neoliberalism, from Adam Smith and John Locke through John Maynard Keynes. The old man bristled when Syd proposed Marx instead, but the two eventually reached a compromise, between the "real" economists and Marx. Only, Syd rewrote their agreement privately, reading the bare minimum of the capitalists in order to make time for all of Marx's *Capital*, volume 1. Caffeinated days and nearly sleepless nights, doubtful musical taste and gems the color of destiny and forlornness — these all chipped away at Syd's ability to discern. He began to feel that everything he read and learned came from one book that explained all that there was to know about cells and exploitation and money and metabolism. Disciplines elided: the decline in the rate of profit was best understood as a natural consequence of lysosomes that broke food down, and mitochondria's need for continuous energy. But continuous energy was not sustainable energy, nor was it synonymous with stasis. Consumption meant growth, always and inevitably growth, and there was no stability where there was growth. It was a common fallacy to believe that the change from adolescence to adulthood entailed a retreat from growth to static maturity, Syd mused one night, tipsy and imagining himself lecturing his priggish economics professor. In truth, those neighborhood girls might arrive at their maximum height by the age of twenty or twenty-one, but they would continue to grow, developing muscle mass and slowly amassing fat deposits on those beautiful hips and breasts and waists, on arms and legs, too. By the age of thirty-five, their faces would grow puffy or plump, or else shed their baby fat as wrinkles affixed permanent evidence of all the laughter and crying that had disrupted the neutrality of their features. In some cases, the stray cancer cells that appear in every human might attain critical mass to become tumors that themselves would grow as long as they could, until stopped either by radiation and surgery and diet, or else death of the host. The cessation of growth occurred at the moment of death. Prior to this, there was only growth, subtle or gross, but in all cases intractable.

And so this decline of the rate of profit was not due to some flaw unique to Capitalism. It was the decline of the rate of thriving, for what used to be enough to support youth and beauty and blossoming was now not enough, would never again be enough. And although he was by now a nominal Marxist, having woken up to the abuses of Capitalism; and although he wanted to right wrongs and thought well enough of the idea of expropriating the expropriators, he was no Marxist at all, he knew in his heart. If he could change anything, it would be the cell's continual need for sustenance, excrescence, and growth. The expropriators are all of us, every single one of us, every cell and every strand of DNA that command us to be avaricious and gluttonous and lustful. If there is guilt, all of us are guilty, because life is guilt.

Annika lay inside of Syd, both in him and of him. What with Syd's feverish state, she imagined herself sitting beside him, his head resting gently on her lap as she smoothed his hair with her fingers. The revelations of the past few hours had uprooted every preconception she had had about Syd, and there was no longer any point in denying what she felt for him. She could also see that she was killing him simply by being inside him, and so she began the process of disengagement, extricating herself from his being until she would come to her senses in her own body. *I'm guilty too*, she thought, already able to suspend herself a few feet above the bed to see Syd's motionless body, his messy hair, the face she had finally been able to see for its beauty and loneliness and stoicism, everything she all at once loved as she had never loved before. *I am guilty too, for I have invaded him. I have violated him in the most fundamental sense. And now I am destroying him.*

She was nearly ready to depart, and Syd was beginning to stir, feeling slightly less weak after his long nap. It was dark outside, and the red clock radio shone 9:28 p.m. Syd flung his arm to the nightstand just as Annika retracted the last of herself from him, just as Syd read the one message from Leta from the whole day, which said, "Is everything alright? Two guys from your lab have been by. Couldn't find you at work, couldn't check to see if you're home. Love you." And, from one of those guys at work: "Call me, it's urgent."

CHAPTER SEVEN
The Emperors

I REMEMBER LITTLE ABOUT MY RETURN from Syd. Sending myself away had always entailed an anti-climactic lull afterward. This time, I was utterly exhausted, and I think it must have been a Friday, because I recall staying in bed for most of the next two days. My skin had a miserable flare-up, and my joints ached even more than they did normally. And then, there was the moment when my bed shook, and because I was sleeping and in pain, that shaking implicated itself into my dream about Bam—Bam of all people!—who was standing at the foot of my bed, appearing in the same sudden, silent way that I appeared when I visited Augustine. So then I understood how unnerving it was to be surprised like that, and, on top of it, Bam was hissing at me, "Don't you think it's time to stop pretending to be good?" repeatedly until it became a nursery rhyme. But my apartment was on the ground floor of a newly constructed building that weathered the earthquake just fine, perhaps thanks to its construction, and perhaps because we, the University of X campus and its environs, were just shy of the sweet spot of the Los Angeles basin, the point at which temblor waves reinforced one another to make it seem like the quake was at least one point higher than its true magnitude. I ignored my computer and phone until Sunday, and only then did I read that Bam's shaking was actually a 7.8-magnitude seism, and that over six hundred people were confirmed dead. I had little time to react, because

Leta wrote to the Eddan mailing list to report that Syd's team had made it possible for the city to avert casualties of a far more serious nature.

When I was later able to get up and move about, I sat at my desk and imagined a new way of relating to Syd, a softer way to make sense of his quirks. Everything about him that I used to resent was now a badge of some hidden honor. He'd have died before letting anyone see those scars of his past. He'd have been mortified to know that I, for whom he justifiably had such contempt, had seen those scars. For what had I ever shown him but distrust? I didn't blame him for loving Leta. No one could have reproached him for that, an opportunity to touch silver moonlight and warmth and darkness all at once. But perhaps he could see that I could be a friend, perhaps as good a friend as Leta, perhaps even closer; for while Leta seemed to be redolent of lunar beauty and mystery, she was nevertheless solar, entirely too solar for the likes of us, Syd and me. Leta was a sun hiding behind the moon. When you are unjustly condemned, when your body is a prison, you know true solitude and coldness. Syd and I knew what it was to live on the wrong side of the moon. And now, here was Syd-the-hero, the warrior who could tame the earth itself. Yes, it was time to reconcile with Syd, perhaps even to meet him again as if for the first time. But there were no opportunities for the next three weeks, what with the disruption of the quake, and the news crews that poured into Syd's lab.

The Dean of the College of Arts and Humanities and Sciences called a meeting for all faculty for 10:00 a.m. the Monday after the earthquake. A full faculty meeting with the Dean was rare, as it was the Dean's primary responsibility to raise funds for the College, and he left faculty governance more or less up to department chairs. The meeting was held in a large lecture hall, and over half of the two hundred seats were filled. The Dean was a tall, lean white man in his fifties. He ran and rowed and biked weekends in those large packs of middle-aged men and women in multicolored spandex outfits that never fit correctly but only accentuated body fat on the flabby and made skinny people look spindly. He was an English literature professor by training, but had entered administration some ten years ago, as soon as he had been promoted to the top of the professoriate. He had two daughters in high school and a wife who was a lawyer for a drug company. He was profoundly content, and most of the faculty thought that he was a good leader. He was a good fundraiser. He dressed well. For this meeting, he was outfitted with a wireless microphone, and the lights were dimmed to accentuate the mild lavender-gray light projected onto the floor-to-ceiling screen at the head of the room. He and his staff clearly had a TED talk in mind as the model for this event.

The Dean was in his element, doing what he was meant to do, perhaps what he was born to do: make people feel good about working, giving money, and dedicating their energy to the university. And as his inspirational speech described the impending restructuring of the College, a talk that made me think of those infomercials I'd have to flip through in order to watch MTV or *Star Trek* reruns late at night when I was in college many years before, what made it possible for me to sit through those two hours and not bolt was to reflect that Roman emperors are, in fact, responsible for corporate culture. If the Republic was Rome's closest attempt at representative democracy, Augustus was the first tyrant to demonstrate how to form committees, and, in so doing, to make the conquered and servile believe that their consent was desired. He asked permission of the Senate before taking control, both he and the Senate knowing full well that Augustus would obtain their blessing with swords if necessary. Augustus went on to be the most beloved of emperors, both during and after his lifetime, and he set the precedent for future autocrats who consulted the toothless Senate in matters of protocol. Just like Augustus, any good subsequent emperor would humbly ask the Senate for the privilege of leading Rome after the Praetorian guard had already installed him. The prototype for all subsequent effete committees, the Senate was content with the perks afforded to its members, swaddled in the fantasy that it held power of any consequence. Gibbon writes:

The successors of Augustus exercised the power of dictating whatever laws their wisdom or caprice might suggest; but those laws were ratified by the sanction of the senate. The model of ancient freedom was preserved in its deliberations and decrees; and wise princes, who respected the prejudices of the Roman people, were in some measure obliged to assume the language and behavior suitable to the general and first magistrate of the republic [. . .] In the exercise of the legislative as well as the executive power, the sovereign advised with his ministers, instead of consulting the great council of the nation. The name of the senate was mentioned with honour till the last period of the empire; the vanity of its members was still flattered with honorary distinctions; but the assembly which had so long been the source, and so long the instrument of power, was respectfully suffered to sink into oblivion. The senate of Rome, losing all connection with the Imperial court and the actual constitution, was left a venerable but useless monument of antiquity on the Capitoline hill.

It was even easier for Diocletian, three centuries after Augustus, to turn the Empire into an overt dictatorship, once he rendered explicit that which, under Augustus, was quietly understood: the Senate was a herd of geldings. Still, Gibbon points out the innovations of Diocletian's reign:

Like the modesty affected by Augustus, the state maintained by Diocletian was a theatrical representation; but it must be confessed, that of the two comedies, the former was of a much more liberal and manly character than the latter. It was the aim of the one to disguise, and the object of the other to display, the unbounded power which the emperors possessed over the Roman world.

And Diocletian's garish, so-called Oriental theater relied on his parading with downcast painted eyes, dressing in colorful silks, parroting the comportment of Persian autocrats who themselves pretended to be gods. In moving the imperial residence east, and eventually to Constantinople, these latter-day emperors further eroded the authority of the Senate. Gibbon was prominent in my thoughts as our Dean ventriloquized both Augustus and Diocletian, as well as Steve Jobs and Elon Musk. After his preliminary statements about the earthquake, he said,

"We're here today to imagine the university of the future. Not the university of the past [here, a slide of Alexander Humboldt appeared on-screen], nor the university that any of us might have attended some years ago."

A low drone faded in on the loud speakers, akin to something that might accompany a trailer for an action film.

"The terrain in higher education is different. We now have to think in terms of competition, whereas before we could content ourselves with abstract or theoretical pursuits. The competition is changing: whereas we used to have to vie with clones of ourselves [here, the coats of arms for the Ivy League universities as well as Stanford], today we need to make the case that attending our school is preferable to an online university or working for a start-up or non-profit.

"How do we do that? How do we make our university a compelling alternative to Harvard? Or to Silicon Valley?

"Before we can answer that, let's consider what Harvard is. Not the Harvard that some of you attended a few decades ago, but the Harvard of today. For Harvard has changed significantly..." [Here, slides of everyone from Mark Zuckerberg and Barack Obama to Henry Louis Gates and Ruth Bader Ginsburg] "... Its faculty and student body are more diverse than ever before. It offers flexibility and rigor at once. And it offers cultural capital, because students who attend Harvard have unlimited access to internships, volunteer work, and nonprofits that, so Harvard reminds us, make the world a better place. Harvard students used to have the reputation of being either rich, or smart, or both. Now, they are still perceived as smart, but they needn't be rich. However, and this part is non-negotiable, they *must* be socially engaged."

He paused to sip from a water bottle. "It's easy to offer the world to students if they are not tied down by curricular red tape. And because Harvard has massive resources, it can afford to offer to students a whole buffet of niche choices, from which any number of idiosyncratic paths can be blazed.

"How do we offer the world to students? How do we offer them what they tell us, time and time again, they want more than anything, the opportunity to be virtuous? This is how."

With that, an appropriately dramatic orchestral music poured in, akin to what might play the moment that a young superhero dons his costume for the first time.

"Starting in Fall 2019, we will offer to students a lighter, more supple curriculum, removing many outdated GE requirements. We will allow greater bandwidth to support electives, in both traditional and online formats, so that students can explore, without having to commit to, any given subject. Finally, we will streamline this transition by taking a hard look at the foundations of a twenty-first-century curriculum, and will consolidate when necessary."

There were murmurs scattered throughout the lecture hall, but the Dean continued, unperturbed.

"What does an English degree mean? I mention English, because I majored in English and went on to become an English professor, so I know that of which I speak. An English degree means that students have taken a list of classes on English literature. Hopefully they've learned how to analyze what they've read, and perhaps they have even learned to write creatively on their own. They certainly have read parts or even all of a whole slew of books. But have they learned anything about what those books describe? Have they learned about kindness..., beauty... [his pauses here were remarkably well-timed] or sacrifice? Have they learned how to share what they have learned with others? Have they learned that what they have learned may not be true, or relevant, for others?

"The quest that our College will now pursue is one that acknowledges that *relevance* [the most skillfully executed italicization I've ever heard] is everything. Relevance to social justice; relevance to future job prospects; and relevance to individual growth..."

He went on for another half-hour or so, but I only listened intermittently. It was clear where this was headed, and the seven-page memo his secretary sent out the next day confirmed it. Majors, as such, were going to be eliminated for everyone but the science majors. There would be no prescribed curricular requirements, only a minimum unit requirement for graduation. And all non-STEM departments would be consolidated, or "united," as the Dean's memo put it, into an entity called Social Relevance Studies, which would contextualize everything from music to law to anthropology, in terms of its *relevance* to students. The Dean's verbal italics were reproduced in the memo, on that pretty word, "relevance." *Relevance.*

That was the Steve Jobs moment, the instant when the visionary leader showed his team how to think outside of the box, disrupt the industry, flip the script, and any number of inane clichés that simply meant doing something showy. But the rest of the Dean's talk and subsequent memo were attempts to forge a false consensus. For, the Dean was careful to repeat at various junctures, this idea was the brainchild of many meetings with a working group chosen from senior faculty across our School. None of my colleagues had heard of such a group, and its membership was never made public. There would be numerous other opportunities for faculty to help shape this initiative, by means of key committees formed to address capstone projects, outreach, fundraising, and curricular redesign. This is a group effort, we were all exhorted to remember, and the participation of everyone was crucial for the success of our School.

I was jolted out of my reverie when the Dean said, "Some of us have already been doing this. Some of us have had the imagination to think about alternatives in higher education. Could we have the folks behind the Center for Critical Studies of Capitalism — Syd Niall and Annika Trent — come down to the stage?" I was dumbstruck. I hadn't dressed up that day, and my face was half-covered with red blotches. It took me a few moments to put down my pen and notebook and tuck in my sloppily thrown-on shirt, and by the time I stood up, Syd was already in front of the audience, smiling and shaking the Dean's hand. The Dean began talking before I reached the stage. "Some of you may already know about the great work that this Center is doing..."

"We prefer the Eddan Collective," I interjected.

"Of course, of course! Thank you, Annika, for that clarification. As I was saying, Syd and Annika's interdisciplinary group is doing wonderful work in a field that it has invented, critical capitalist studies..."

Syd guffawed, and I sputtered, "...critical studies of Capitalism, and we hardly invented it."

The Dean looked at me, his smile unflappable, but his eyes had hardened. He was not used to being corrected in public. "Right, right. One of the perks of this job is that I get to learn from my wonderful faculty. I guess you'd say that I'm a life-long learner! At any rate, I'm sure that no one in this room needs to be reminded of the critical, lifesaving work that Syd and his team have done, work that helped avert what could have been a catastrophe. I'm speaking of course of the recent earthquake, but we should keep in mind that this work is only at its beginning stages, and will hopefully be useful in future seismic events.

"Syd and Annika's group, however it is called (and who knows? You may decide to change your name to something snappier after you hear this announcement) is a model for our School, because it has embraced interdisciplinarity as a point of departure for a very real, basic, and *relevant* problem: how do we predict the next catastrophe, whether seismic or economic? This is a project-based initiative that starts with a problem, and adapts curriculum to the needs of the problem-solvers. In a certain sense, you have to love the problem more than anything else in order to excel at this job.

"It is for these reasons that the Provost and I have agreed to award Syd's group $1 million as a seed grant to pursue larger external funds. We hope that this group's success will serve to galvanize other cross-disciplinary initiatives that have *relevance* as their point of departure."

There was the requisite applause, and then a few concluding remarks, and then the meeting ended — without a question-and-answer period. The Dean was quick to approach Syd and me, and after publicly shaking our hands while the School's photographer snapped away, he asked for a word in his office. We walked there together, none of us saying anything. Once inside the office, the Dean threw down his shoulder bag and coat, and his administrator's smile faded. He said softly,

"Annika, never contradict me in public again," and glared at me for an instant before composing himself and turning to Syd. "Now, Syd, I'm sorry for not giving you advanced warning about the grant. The funding just came through this morning, and I didn't want to miss an opportunity to attach the good news to the re-org."

"Thank you, Dave, but Annika's the co-director, you should address her as well."

"I was. I am."

"Good . . . Dave, that interdisciplinary grant I applied for a few months ago — that was for a million dollars."

"Yes."

"Is the money you're giving us really that grant?"

"Yes."

"So, you're not actually using School funds to pay us. It's the Provost's money."

"Yes."

I jumped in, "But you presented it as if it were the School's funds."

"Yes." The Dean sat down on the sofa adjacent to the conference table, and motioned for us to sit down on two chairs facing him. "Here's the situation. The university is in trouble. Big trouble. We will be freezing all new hires for the next year. We anticipate that freshmen enrollments will be down 40% versus where they were two years ago. We'll be reinstating the accelerated retirement incentives program to get folks out as soon as we can. We are suspending employer contributions to retirement plans. We are going into survival mode."

Syd said, "This seems a bit dramatic. We've heard the predictions about a gradual decline, but this seems fast."

"Oh, it's been coming for a while. We have all those competitors I mentioned: online for-profits; online state schools; the old cadre of prestige colleges. We have the job market, too; high school students are seeing the shitty jobs that await the majority of college graduates. Some of them know that the global food chain will collapse in fifteen years. Why go to college if there won't be enough to eat in a few decades? Quite simply, the kids don't want our product anymore; neither do their parents. And they do want to look and feel virtuous."

I was able to interject, "So what will happen?"

"For a time, things will appear normal, especially since the STEM students will continue as before. But no more English or history majors, just kids who take English and history or any other kind of elective they like."

"So why are you telling us this?" Syd asked.

"Because you need to know how dire the situation is, so that you can preach the good news of the re-org. The faculty will be up in arms when they see the scope of the changes in store for them. I would, too, if I weren't the fool who agreed to run things. If you in your leadership positions can act as a calming influence, it will help morale, perhaps even dissuade those contemplating a strike. You can buy us time."

I asked, "Buy time for what?"

"To get us all an extra five, maybe ten years. Don't think that this is a predicament unique to the University of X. It's the same across North America. Those of us who set our sights on the professoriate as a career, those of us who are humanists, mind you, for the scientists can always find work in industry—we can talk all day about the utility of a Ph.D. outside academia, but who are we fooling? We went into this line of work because we fell in love, at an impressionable age, with reading books, with writing poetry, with singing, with studying dead languages. Becoming speech-writers, consultants, real estate agents, or high school teachers is not an acceptable alternative, but it's all that most of us, me included, could reasonably hope to do."

Syd sighed and mumbled, "There's a certain nobility in that, I suppose."

I said, "But you are completely caving to the economic model. The university is supposed to be a sanctuary from Capitalism and hegemony, and you are turning it into a stable for grooming future capitalists and wage slaves."

As the Dean began to respond to me, the light in the room dimmed, and the Dean's business suit clouded over and became purple robes, and the Dean's face changed, into something smaller, more angular, darker. He was no longer an urbane, self-aware administrator, trying to save himself and his friends on a sinking ship. Now he was Emperor Constantine at the moment when he threw in his lot with the Christians and moved the capital of the Empire east, from Rome to the city upon which he forced his name. And in the flickering light that danced on the walls in a room now illuminated by braziers, with the air now heavy with incense, Syd's face conveyed no surprise, and I knew that only I could see the Emperor, that I had sent myself away, again without meaning to do so. The Emperor looked at me sternly and said that there was no hope for Rome or the pagans, that the only future was one where Christ would protect his own under his standard, where soldiers of Christ would cut everything that stood in the way of union with the Bride Church. It was Constantine, after all, who would perfect bureaucracy far beyond what even Augustine or Diocletian had done, setting in place a system that would last two thousand years, that would stifle opposition before it could take root. I shook my head and said that Christ would have had nothing to do with this, and I moaned that his institution of the clergy as a separate jurisdiction, subject to no civil laws and all but explicitly empowered to cover up and silence scandals, would make it possible for priests to commit any number of abuses with impunity. And Constantine said that it was in the hands of Christ now, that he would protect the innocent, and he admonished me not to say a word to Syd, for Syd was not yet ready to see him as he really was. And Syd looked at me oddly and said, "It's alright,

Annika, we'll work this out later, let's go," and I was then standing and pointing and yelling until Syd all but shoved me outside and I saw the Dean's face before Syd slammed the door after us, and his eyes caught mine and he saw that I knew, that he was Constantine and we were the Christians, now being elevated to undreamt-of power at the expense of our souls.

Syd held my arm as he walked us to the elevator. He let me go once the doors slid shut, but said, "I'll call security if you try to go back up."

I was breathing heavily.

"We're going to sit down, you and I, and have a talk about all of this."

"Whatever you like, just don't touch my arm. It hurts."

He flinched and quickly apologized, saying that he didn't realize he had hurt me.

"You didn't do anything wrong; it's just that my skin breaks out in welts, and it hurts anytime something touches me."

He led me across a few streets to his apartment, and upon opening the door he asked, "Leta?", and, hearing no reply, he threw down his bag on the sofa and said, "I'll make tea."

I didn't know how to act, entering an apartment that I was supposed not to have seen before. I sank down into the closest chair. He brought out the tea after a few minutes, and asked about my skin. I told him what the doctors had told me, that my condition had no name because it exhibited traits of several conditions: lupus, psoriasis, fibromyalgia, chronic myeloid leukemia. But a little of each of these sicknesses did not add up to a comprehensible whole. My ailment was nameless. Syd chuckled and said that the current state of global affairs was in a similar predicament. The word "Capitalism" didn't encompass the symptoms of our malaise. "And without a name, it's difficult to know what we're fighting."

He paused for some moments, and not looking at me, eventually said, "I'm sincerely sorry for how I've behaved toward you. Most of what hasn't worked between us has been due to me."

I didn't look at him, didn't move, didn't dare to react. He continued, "And I had no idea that you were contending with these physical issues. Typical me, assuming that I am the center of the universe." He chuckled nervously. Still I said nothing, but I was beginning to feel warm, not like I do during a flare-up, but as I hadn't felt since I was young and used to fall asleep lying on the beach. The warmth was sweet and strong and reassuring.

"So please take what I'm about to say as something meant with kindness. Something coming from a friend, if you'd accept a friend as unfriendly as I have been."

I finally looked at him, daring to wish what I had wished all along.

"I think you should step down from the Eddans."

I had started to smile as he had spoken of kindness and friendship, and so it was with the smile of an idiot that I listened to his ensuing words.

"Annika, what just happened in Dave's office . . . that was serious. That can't happen ever again. I don't know what else you're contending with—it's none of my business—but I can't rely on you to keep your composure."

I swallowed, and the warmth began to seep out of my body.

"The man just gave us a million dollars, and you can't simply bite your tongue and say 'Thank you'?"

The smile began to fade, too, only my lips trembled as the facial muscles relaxed. I must have looked as if I might have a seizure, but Syd was looking into his hands, his elbows perched on his knees.

"I don't have the slightest notion of what you were saying in there. And I do want to understand you—I want to be your friend—so I must tell you when I see you going off the rails. You need help, not from me but from a professional. And I cannot let you jeopardize what we've both worked so hard to achieve."

I was now looking down, attempting to still my cheeks, looking like I was smiling or about to break up with laughter. But I said nothing, and Syd waited until he couldn't stand it any longer.

"So . . . do you have anything to say? What do you think?"

The words came to me, though I had no means of reflecting on them. "The disaster for which you've spent your life preparing is coming, but you'll be able to do nothing to avoid it."

"What?"

"By trying to control that disaster, you have pushed it into areas even more threatening, more noxious."

Syd was back to his normal disdainful manner, rolling his eyes and checking his messages. But this flippancy in turn dissipated as I continued to speak.

"Syd, I have seen you. I know about your mother and her sense of guilt after the deaths of her mother and sister. I know about those neighborhood girls of summer, how you fell in love with their beauty before you knew what beauty or love were. And I know how you were condemned. You now manage your risks, and you play the part of someone contemptible because you can manage that role with detachment. But I also know about the linarite, and how your father introduced you to the first love of your life, that impossible blue for which you've searched ever since. So, you see, there is nothing sick about me, nothing at all. I may need to hold my tongue, as you say — yes, of course, I can learn to play that game — but you needn't worry about me, for I know more about you than do your family, your lover, or anyone else. For I love you more than anyone. Yes, Syd, I love you for who you are beneath your lies and hostilities and arrogance. I love you for your innocence. And I must stay on with the Eddans, you see, because you and I are supposed to work together. You know it's true. I am the *malayka*, and you are the dragon, and if we simply leave these bodies behind, we can start the real work of saving our world from itself, of finding a new way to live. Remember? Those were your words. We can do it, because I love you so very much . . ."

Syd was looking at me, his face ashen and his jaw slack. He is seeing me for the first time, I remember thinking giddily. But then he groaned—it was the most awful sound I have ever heard—and he stood in front of me and threw me down onto the floor, and he hit me with his open hands, then he clenched his hands into fists and beat my face and chest, and I was too surprised to move, and I wished that he might kiss me, but he just hit me, and he eventually stopped when he seemed to realize that I was bleeding from the mouth and nose. And then he rolled off of me and began to sob, and moved to a corner of the room, and he wept, and I sat up and tried to approach him, and he groaned, "If you try to touch me, I'll break your neck." Some time passed, I cannot be sure how much, only that I sat back on the sofa and dozed off, perhaps he did too, and then later he got up and went into the bathroom and locked the door, and through it he said softly, "If you're still here when I come out, I'm calling the police." And I left, and felt nothing as I returned home and looked in the mirror at the red bruises on my face that were already starting to turn purple. I felt nothing, because I was still hearing him sob, and could not understand why he did not kiss me. It must have been a misunderstanding, I kept saying. After all, I told him that he was innocent.

It was another three weeks from the Dean's meeting to the next Eddans meeting. Syd didn't call the meeting; rather, it was Leta, and she invited us all to her studio for a presentation of her new composition, as well as a discussion of the next steps in the wake of our newly acquired support. I was nervous, to say the least, about seeing Syd again, and assumed that he would have told Leta about our conversation with the Dean, and our subsequent . . . private conversation. But Syd didn't show up, and Leta seemed as friendly as usual, just nervous before playing her music in front of the group. She said to all of us, "Syd called this meeting but has since needed to go out of town, and there's no agenda. I'm selfishly asking if I could play you what I've been working on. It may be relevant to this group . . ." She giggled a little, and, seeing no objection, she sat down among the synthesizers and consoles and interfaces scattered on the floor to one side of the studio, and began the music. It wasn't a live performance, of course, yet it was live, for she played a recording, and also played guitar to accompany that recording. I cringe at reading what I just wrote, because I know that there must be a better way to describe all of this. Leta could help me, I suppose. The music was both consistent with her previous work, and unlike anything I had ever heard. The distortion and echoes that were so familiar from Leta's mixed media piece were there, but it was as if she had transplanted them to fifth-century Hippo. There were cymbals and a high-pitched, nasal-sounding wind instrument, something like an oboe but more insistent. And there was the little theme, the same fragment that I had heard when I sent myself away to Hippo, when I spoke to the man holding his dying mother, the man who called me a *malayka*. There was no way that Leta could have known about that melody, no means for her to have been present the day that I was called a *malayka* by Augustine and the grieving man and the dragon. And yet here was that little tune, and I looked hard at Leta to see if she was not a witch or demon or perhaps even a *malayka* herself, someone who could send herself away as I could. But Leta did not look up during the performance. She seemed genuinely engrossed and did not once catch my eye or wink or otherwise communicate knowing or irony.

The music continued, and I heard in it scenes both intimate and epic. The son grieved for his mother, and rejoiced in her deliverance from suffering. And yet an army approached, one that originated far to the north, in air that stung the face and throat with frost. The army was hardly an army in any contemporary sense, but rather a mob of lost ravenous fists and mouths. They ransacked with their eyes even before they could break anything, and they forced a march that would relentlessly overtake Rome, Gaul, even Hippo. I looked across the room as Leta's music continued, and I caught Philip's eyes — Philip, my former student who was now playing the revolutionary with grownups in their little club. But Philip was no longer a callow adolescent, but instead heard and saw what I heard and saw. We looked together at the bearded northerners who were scanning the ground for grain, tools, anything, staring with open mouths if a girl or woman was unfortunate enough to approach. Philip's voice whispered in my ear, "Only a dragon could take them down."

"There is no dragon here," I said with regret.

"You wouldn't recognize a dragon if it stood before you. But don't doubt, a dragon is the answer."

I must have nodded off during Leta's performance, and when I came to, Philip was standing in front of the Eddans, speaking normally and saying nothing about the army or dragons.

"Thank you, Leta. That was beyond gorgeous. I'm not sure anyone could follow that!" Laughter scattered about the room. "Um, like, since you invited us to speak about the next steps, I wanted to say that I'm super excited to begin work on Marx, and other relevant authors."

Again, scattered responses throughout the room, mostly sounds of vigorous agreement. Someone in the back called out, "Yeah, I was wondering when we'd get around to the critique-of-Capitalism part of this critical-studies-of-Capitalism group." Several others laughed.

"Hmm, yes, right . . . ," I began. "Thank you, Philip, for your kind words." I mumbled a few more pleasantries, demolished by the glaring truth that this little club was a joke. I went on to say that Marx had comprehensively studied and documented every aspect of Capitalism. "Any clearheaded consideration would have to admit that capitalists would never allow the revolution. This explains why every subsequent attempt at large-scale communism failed: because Capitalism or hegemonic thought inevitably infiltrated the system. There has never been any such thing as communism."

There were a few grumbling sounds from the audience, but I went on. I recall clearly that I figured I might as well lay out all my thoughts now, perhaps the only opportunity I'd have before Syd returned. I paused, found an open space amid the various synthesizers and control boxes and electric guitars that littered the floor, and sat down with my legs crossed. I remember continuing to speak even as the vision of the advancing army returned to me. For I was now sitting among the soldiers as they walked past me, sometimes stumbling to avoid walking on me. Their breath was putrid, and they looked upon me with hatred, even fear, but they did not stop their march, and they did not try to accost me. I began to speak of the schism between essence and teleology, a pivot from Plato to Aristotle that forever condemned their descendants to think of the goal, the final destination, for any invention or enterprise. We are incapable of experiencing anything without considering its ramifications. How long will the thing last? How much will it cost or earn? Will it get better or worse?

As I was asking these rhetorical questions, I was dimly aware of my gesturing to amplify the meaning of my words, but I thought nothing of it, as I usually spoke with my hands.

"Now, these questions are pernicious enough on their own, since they already contain the soul of human unhappiness, the restlessness that will be our scourge as long as our species persists. But when these questions appear in the minds of capitalists, there is the additional tragedy that they don't simply remain mute talismans of anxiety. To the contrary, these questions spur concrete actions. The successful businessman who already enjoys dominance over a market, but who seeks to drive out his competitor, simply because static coexistence is not enough. The corporation that seeks to triple its already impressive profits, because shareholders always want more. So, the present is forever linked to the future, to multiple futures either terrifying or impoverished or prosperous, depending on whether the right action is taken in the present.

"What an awful responsibility to place on the shoulders of the present!" I said, pausing for dramatic effect as I held my arms above my head. I thought that my gestures were a little cheesy, but didn't bother too much about it. After all, no one would care what I thought.

"I want to return to Marx, in order to disagree with him. He has given us so much, but that doesn't mean that we side with the capitalists if we critique him. I want to consider Marx's comments in the Introduction of the *Grundrisse*. In one concluding passage, he says that while older art works like the *Iliad* afford us great aesthetic pleasure, we can never return to the social conditions and mythology that made the *Iliad* possible. True enough, but he ends with a tirade against 'the old peoples,' primitive cultures like that of Classical Greece that contained 'unripe social conditions.' Marx may have inherited a lot from Hegel, but he rejected the immanence of Spirit, which is the very premise of Hegel's system. That which is constant in Marx's system is class division, not Spirit. Because of this, Marx rejects stasis, cycles, and even attempts to avoid the teleology of Capitalism, like hoarding. To quote Marx from later in *Grundrisse*, 'Economy of time, to this all economy ultimately reduces itself.' That is, Marx himself is utterly shackled to time, to teleology. The present moment is, for Capitalism and for capitalists' greatest gadfly, never untethered to the future.

"So let us envision now an utter break from teleology and the awful weight of this 'economy of time.' If you will, let us pretend that we are innocent angels from Blake. We can turn away from teleology, toward cycles and stasis."

As I was speaking, the army returned, only now I could simultaneously see the Eddan members. They were standing or sitting on the same barren landscape as I was, and the soldiers were passing us by. I must have concluded that the Eddans could see the soldiers, for the soldiers saw the Eddans, curling their lips at the effete scholar-mendicants who did nothing even as the world was collapsing.

"We can avoid getting caught up in their violence by sticking to the earth, by returning again and again to the earth, to earth's time and rhythms. For we cannot escape. Capitalism's greatest failure is its inability to achieve balance, composure, sustainability—whatever words you choose to represent stasis. If any of you were to stand up right now and begin to worry about the decline, if you were to try to stave it off, to meddle in this economy of time, the soldiers would cut you down like wheat."

There were a few muffled sounds from the other members, but I couldn't make out any words.

"Please join me in making the Eddans a research center for cycles, for stasis. We may not be able to ignite a revolution in the traditional sense. But we can turn our own lives into beacons for stasis. We can refuse to be reduced to an economy of time, if we disable the very idea of economy."

I ran out of things to say. Philip looked at me with a blank expression. Leta winced, as if she were embarrassed to be seen with me. There was a vacuum in the room, and a few people shifted uncomfortably. The voice that had cracked the joke about critiquing Capitalism spoke again, and I strained to see that it was Bam, and that the disdain I heard in his voice was altogether absent. Bam said, "I for one am very energized by your performance, Annika. You point the way forward to an absurdist-yet-utopian manner of play, one that is philosophically grounded yet that enfranchises rather than obfuscates. This is a neo-Dadaist platform for opting out of Capitalism. I like it!" Bam spoke without a hint of irony, but there was a light in his eye that seemed off somehow. I wanted to cry out that this was no performance art piece, that I wasn't playing at anything, but that I was simply speaking from the heart. But I was too slow in responding, and others in the meantime were nodding in agreement, especially Leta, who seemed to have recovered from her mortification.

"I couldn't agree more. Annika, this is so original, and yet so simple. You have empowered us to become so many Bartlebies, but not the Bartleby who mopes and pouts. No, this Bartleby drops out joyfully, and infuses an ecological levity that deflates every naysayer."

I glared at Leta and said, "Bartleby wasn't a pouter." But few people heard me, since the room started to boil over with chatter. Those who did hear me lash out, including Leta herself, thought that my speech was an act and that I was still in character. They laughed nervously. Bam caught my eye. He was still sitting at the back of the room, and nodding with satisfaction. Leta eventually called the room to order, and proceeded to ask for suggestions for the next action items. Two committees were formed. Leta nominated me as chair of one of the committees, called the Breakout Group for Performance Conceptualization. The other group, called the Theoretical Grounding of Aesthetic Gestures Subgroup, was populated by three people I had never met. I left early, and no one noticed.

CHAPTER EIGHT
Bartleby

I COULD HAVE BEEN FURIOUS ABOUT ANY number of things that had happened at that meeting, but now, with the ineluctable dust of forgetfulness that has accumulated on my memories, I recall only that my greatest vitriol was reserved for Leta's invocation of Herman Melville's short story, *Bartleby, the Scrivener*. Like many Leftists of the era, Leta saw in the character of Bartleby a heroic symbol of what was wrong with Capitalism, and how to cure that ailment. For Bartleby was the copyist, recently hired in a profitable law firm, whose previous employment was in a dead-letter office. Bartleby's "quiet desperation" (to paraphrase Melville's peer Thoreau's famous phrase) led him one day to stage the most effective of labor strikes. When asked by his employer and colleagues why he was not at his appointed task, he responded, "I prefer not to." And thus he responded to every subsequent invitation, request, and order, until he was imprisoned, refused to eat, and starved himself to death.

Leta's casual assertion that Bartleby was a "pouter" unnerved me. The famous Slavoj Žižek, the hero of Leta's cohort, had a T-shirt made with that little quote, now a mantra for the Left. "I prefer not to" became an impossibly capacious reservoir for innumerable acts of heroic disobedience. I prefer not to mow the lawn, pay my taxes, vote in the next election, participate in a neoliberal economy that reduces everyone and everything to an exploitable material or service. I prefer not to protest, I prefer not to hope. I prefer not to admit that, in writing this passage, I am cribbing from the Irvine Welsh novel, *Trainspotting*. Above all, I prefer not to have a better idea, for a better world and better way of doing things. And so, while I loved Bartleby (for he was the earliest of the idealists with whom I would fall in love during my adolescence, to be followed by Rodion Romanovitch Raskolnikov and Quentin Compson), I despised what my supposedly kindred spirits of the Left saw in him. To them, he meant nothing, literally, just a smug way of divesting the invoker of any responsibility.

I was thinking noxious thoughts of this nature while walking home, and, without noticing precisely when it began, at some point Bartleby appeared, walking alongside me and displaying an uncharacteristic absorption in me. I had seen him before, a tall thin man in his late twenties, bookish and not particularly well-nourished or vital. I had loved him for that self-forgetting so many years ago. But that type of love had been safe, for I could then see Bartleby without him seeing me, and I was free to love in an entirely hopeless manner, knowing that my love would never be returned. Now, I looked upon him anxiously, for I had in the intervening years fallen in love with someone else, equally inaccessible and far angrier, and didn't know how to respond to the care in his gaze.

"What are you going on about?" he asked.

"What do you mean?"

"Well, here you are, railing against that poor woman, acting like you know what I meant."

"What you meant?" I trailed off, incredulous.

"What I meant when I was lost and used to say hopeless things."

This was indeed Bartleby before me, but nothing in his words or bearing jibed with what I knew or recognized. This was a completely different person, no longer a victim of quiet desperation, no longer a standard bearer for resignation. I turned my eyes away; I swiveled my head straight ahead and walked faster, but he kept up with me just the same.

"You shouldn't hold it against her," he continued. "People need a hero, and I guess that she's so smart that she knows there's no solution. So, she looks for a hero who tells her that it's acceptable not to search for a solution."

"Hang on right there," I growled. We were no longer on campus or near my apartment, or anywhere in Los Angeles. We were walking on a small, unpaved service road that circled the research institute a quarter-mile away from the residence where I lived during graduate school. It was late spring, and the ground was blanketed with a thick grass, longer and wider than any of the straw that grows in California. When I was a student, that fragrance of grass was intoxicating, a completely unknown delight to someone who had come from the West. It was sweet and young and almost obsessive in its persistence. I kept analyzing each of my inhalations, attempting to determine whether I had imagined a scent so devoid of imperfections. My heart soared to be back in the town of my graduate school with that fragrance; but, again, something was off, perhaps something so basic as the fact that I never spent time rereading *Bartleby the Scrivener* in graduate school. And thus, if I had never read of Bartleby while at graduate school, then Bartleby didn't belong here in this bucolic little town; and, therefore, I didn't belong here either.

"Let me get this straight," I said. "You think that I'm being too hard on Leta. But you also agree with me, that she is using your refusals to justify her own desires."

"That's about right." His eyes softened, and I only then saw some of the sweetness I would have attributed to him long ago.

"So what is your solution? Should you, Bartleby, be a cipher for every discontented Leftist and intellectual?

How about me? I prefer not to forgive that silly fool. I prefer not to show her compassion for invoking you. I prefer not to forgive her for taking Syd away from me, before I even had a chance . . . "

I broke off, sobbing, and Bartleby put his hand on my shoulder and guided me away from the service road and toward the Institute, where there were a few benches scattered on the lawns shaded under great magnolia trees. I sobbed some more and then calmed down enough to say, "We shouldn't be here. How are we here and not in LA?"

"How, indeed? And you could have started with a better question yet: how is it that you are speaking to a fictional character? Or, how can you send yourself away, to people who died several centuries ago? Or, let's go further: how could you possibly know such intimate details about Syd? For that is really why you're in such a state, isn't it? Leta has her hands on the man you now love, and then she mentioned me, a man you used to love. Isn't that right?"

I stared at the ground in silence.

"Annika, I don't understand this any more than you do. So I can only speak of things I do know. The first being that, as soon as I died, the moment I said my last 'I prefer not to' and let go of everything, I went to Hell."

Something in the way Bartleby said this was so abrupt and dispassionate that I couldn't stop myself from giggling. I stifled it quickly, but Bartleby heard me and paused, a wounded look in his eyes. Still, he continued:

"The Hell to which I descended was not the Hell I expected. No brimstone, no fire. It was, in fact, the Hell of Melville's creation, and I was chained to a ship-wreck at the bottom of the ocean, looking up as the Pequod was hunting whales. At some moments, Moby Dick was present, but at other times, the Pequod was chasing other creatures, and I could see Queequeg and

Tashtego and Daggoo flinging their harpoons like lances, and Ishmael looking on in wonder. For I had been imbued, upon the moment of my death, with a thorough knowledge of Melville's writings. His universe, his creations, everything he set down on paper. It makes sense from a certain point of view, since I was one of those creations. At any rate, there I was, watching the saga of *Moby Dick* again and again, shackled to some wreck at the bottom that was not quite deep enough to obscure the deeds of those on the surface. I watched, in silence and torment."

He looked at me, took in the questioning in my eyes. "I understand your confusion," he went on. "What was the nature of this hell?, you wonder. Was it physical pain? Was I in agony? Agony, yes, but an agony of the spirit rather than the body. For I suffered because I saw the actions of others, actions that were noble and bold, actions that affirmed. I spent the best part of my life preferring not to do anything. And now, as I saw the Pequod and its whaling boats skid across the sea's surface, backlit with a solar disk that was nowhere near searing from the vantage point of the bottom of the ocean, I saw that preferring not to live was its own punishment."

I looked across the grass in front of the Institute's main entrance. It was odd to see a lawn so well-tended amid natural greenery that was even healthier in appearance. A Californian like me contemplates green landscaping with a twinge of guilt. For green grass in a desert is possible only through irrigation, and irrigation demands investments of money and infrastructure. And in a drought environment where every drop is spoken for, green lawns imply a subtle rebuke of the community, one's neighbors, and life itself. This is a roundabout way of explaining why this greener-than-green lawn at the Institute was so odd. It rained regularly in this small town, especially in the spring, so there was no water shortage. The forest that encircled the Institute and came up to its very doorstep was thriving. Anything could have grown here, and without help. Yet even as Bartleby disclosed the monstrosity of his postmortem existence, the sprinklers turned on automatically, and the preternaturally green lawn for which its upkeep deprived no one of water basked in its surfeit. I felt ashamed even though there was no need for guilt. And so I felt toward Bartleby, whose change of heart seemed *off*, no matter how sincerely he spoke. There was certainly no need for him to regret his former life of demurral. I had no need for motivational speeches. But I saw a small-souled man who gave in, perhaps to his own conscience disguised as his God-as-Melville, who meted out punishment to his disobedient children.

Bartleby was evidently endowed with the ability to read my mind, for he responded to my unspoken thoughts directly: "You despise me for giving in. You would rather have me as I was, a pathetic conscientious objector, than as I am now, someone who prefers affirmation to negation. I would prefer now to live, although that privilege is no longer mine. And you, you who claim to love me," his voice dropped to a whisper as he caressed my cheek, "would prefer me as lost and belonging to you, rather than found and liberated."

He said this with no hint of recrimination. His voice was soft and kind like the lover I dreamt of. And it dropped further in volume as he said, barely audibly, "You are ill, Annika. Your illness is spreading. It used to plague only your body, but now it is overtaking your soul. You, who thought yourself innocent and well-meaning. You, who hid from outside evil, are fairly covered with it, with ragged feathers and putrescent wings."

He turned his gaze from me to the overwatered lawn, and continued, "And, no, I have not disguised Melville as my own conscience. Yes," he responded to my questioning look, "I can read your thoughts. You think that

I have given in. But you haven't been listening, which is surprising, coming from a Marxist. Let me repeat this, in case you didn't hear." His words were low and gentle: "I am in Hell. You fail to draw the logical conclusion, so I will spell it out. God exists. And I rejected His mercy. In my despair, I let the material world destroy me, because I thought that the material world was all that there is. Don't make that mistake, Annika."

CHAPTER NINE
The Spinning Compass

ROUND SPUN THE COMPASS NEEDLE, NOT stopping, never. Not even in my anger with the Eddans, the Dean, and Leta. Nor during my sullen adoration of Syd. Ideologies became interchangeable and disposable. Marxism, free market Capitalism, nihilism, Catholicism, esotericism, atheism—I careened amid them all.

A few weeks after the Eddans meeting and the ensuing, bewildering conversation with Bartleby, my doctor called me. And I showed up for the appointment that he had recommended, or rather, the one his nurse called to recommend, since he never made calls, no doctors did; the exigencies of "managed care" were such that doctors were too busy to call their own patients. And I sat on the bed, with goosebumps from the cold, waiting in the paper gown that is supposed to allow the doctor better access for performing an examination. Only there was no need for examination, for the doctor and I both knew everything there was to know about my sickness from the blood tests he had me take every two weeks, and from the biopsies I underwent annually. I was wearing something useless in that it kept me neither modest nor warm. I smiled to myself, that I was literally wearing an absurdity. And I smiled also because I could see what was coming, the scene in a mediocre film when a character receives a grim prognosis, and must now come to terms with mortality. I imagined poignant, tasteful piano music to underscore the moment when the doctor tells me that my sky-high blood counts, higher than in any healthy person, had started a gradual but consistent descent around ten months ago. And he'd continue that this was, far from being a sign of remission or healing, an indication of disease progression. And in that bad movie, there would be a close-up shot of my face in profile, staring blankly ahead as the implications of a much-sooner-than-expected death begin to sink in.

Only I had already seen this bad movie, and I had already read up on what declining hemoglobin levels portend. And I left the doctor's office, not scared or depressed, but with an urge to buy something. For when the compass spins and the ship has lost its bearings, it is not that there is no true north. Rather, there are any number of norths, all momentarily attracting the needle, making it pause almost thoughtfully before resuming its senseless gyrations. In those days around the time that the Eddans formed, I chased thrills in the minor occult—nothing serious like witchcraft or satanism, mind you—just lukewarm excursions that promised a shudder of esoteric delight. I had taken up tarot several months before, and I bought a new tarot deck whenever I wanted distraction. So it was with no hesitation that I went home and bought online a reproduction of a deck that I had long coveted, the Viéville Tarot from around the year 1650. With expedited shipping from an outlet in Bulgaria, I'd have the deck within five days.

What brought me to tarot in the first place was a desire for a better prognosticator. For with my unnamed illness giving regular signs since my mid-twenties that my body would deteriorate, and with the researchers of mysterious conditions such as mine acquiring more data on lifespans and quality-of-life, I had developed the habit of consulting the online calculators, in greater abundance with each passing year, that divined what time I had left based on my blood counts and mutational status. There were a few available, with acronyms like IPSS and DIPSS. The "PSS" meant "prognostic scoring system," and assigned points based on a few criteria, like anemia and counts of immature blood cells and spleen enlargement. Depending on the algorithm, I had between five and ten years. All models agreed that the first half of what time remained would be roughly normal, and that I would experience significant symptoms of constitutional decline during the second half. The phrase "constitutional decline" always made me chuckle. Would the University of X experience night sweats and enlarged spleen, given that it was, like me, undergoing constitutional decline? Wasn't the United States in a state of constitutional decline? And when the joke had run its course, I reproached myself for being so engrossed with these exaggerated rumors of my imminent demise. It wasn't as if I had an inoperable tumor with only six months left to live. So why did I feel so sorry for myself? I upbraided myself with thoughts such as, *I should regard this illness as a gift, an opportunity to put my priorities in order; perhaps let go of the Eddans and Syd; forgive Leta; pour myself into teaching; read any of the books I have been eager to devour; pray; make peace with God,* and any number of other noble projects.

But, no. Instead, I'd return to the calculators, updating my time-remaining after every new blood test and bone marrow biopsy, a procedure in which a nurse stuck a syringe into my pelvis from the back to extract marrow, while I lay on my side and screamed into a towel. My doctor relied on the DIPSS as he might an oracle, and spent less time translating for me what he saw on the slides of my smeared marrow samples than demonstrating the mysterious calculator on his screen that told him whether I fell into low, intermediate, or high risk categories. Then I started to visit those oracle-calculators as well, at first every month or so, then weekly and then finally daily, even multiple times a day, changing variables slightly to see what bearing a small change in my blast count or spleen size would have on my time remaining. One day I happened to see a tarot deck in a movie, sometime around a year before I met Syd, and it reminded me that I had always wanted to have a tarot deck, ever since I was a little girl, only I hadn't known where to find one or how to learn the meaning of the cards. Tarot decks would certainly not make me scream into a towel, I thought. I bought my first deck, a Rider Waite, and spent the next week drawing three cards at a time — never more than that, I had no interest in Celtic crosses or seashells or any other, more elaborate spreads — and learning the symbols. And I loved those images by Pamela Colman; I treasured the sense of alarm in the sword pips, the faux-medieval pageantry of the cups, the hieratic forbidding of the major arcana. But those Rider Waite cards, as much as I cherished them, did little for me; for what could their Arthurian cartoon characters tell me about mutational status, or signs of constitutional decline, in either me or the university? So I moved on from the gateway drug of the Rider Waite to obscurer decks: the Marseille tarots, including the Noblet, Dodal, and Payen; the even older anonymous Tarot de Paris, which anticipated cubism's butchering of the face and body; the twentieth-century Gran Tarot Esoterico, whose major arcana refer to Basque mythology but whose pips are as unforthcoming and tantalizing as the Marseille decks.

These more elusive decks gave me less, which paradoxically made me consult them more than those prognosticator apps. For now, I was no longer thinking about how much time I had left, but instead struggled to relate distinct cards, arbitrary pips from seemingly inert suits and majors that seemed above any commotion amongst those pips. Tarot made sense of the atomized and arbitrary in daily life. When my skin underwent a particularly aggressive flare-up, any bâton card would indicate fire, and a number, the severity and duration of the episode. An unpleasant day at work could be rationalized through the intercession of the face cards: kings were the bosses, queens the managers, knights the zealots, and valets, inevitably me in my naïveté. While the tiny voice of my conscience chided me for giving into superstition and wasting whatever time I had left, it was only a tiny voice, and tarot's louder and more persuasive voice made me feel better than I had felt in a long time, even better than when I sent myself away, for I had blemished that activity by desecrating Syd. Tarot was, at least for the time being, like innocence itself.

Jacques Viéville was a "master card maker" based in Paris between 1643 and 1664. Viéville's deck, the deck that arrived less than a week after the doctor told me that my bone marrow was drying up, featured only a few predominant colors: black, red, gold, and a noncommittal green that was a mixture of black and gold. The images were well-drawn and better than in other decks from the same period. They were far from master etchings like those of Dürer, but they could suggest doubt, reticence, and lust as clearly as any decent Renaissance painting. That said, their quality was disconcertingly uneven — for all the poise in a face card's visage, the clothing on the very same card appeared as flat and nonsensical, like an Escher sketch only started but not fleshed out. Still, these cards were dearer to me than any others. Tarot historians insist that these early decks had never been intended for divination, that all of that esoteric business only came later, in the build-up to the French Revolution, as the Enlightenment gave voice to its private terror at the hands of so-called reason. This meant that we are supposed to accept seventeenth-century decks at face value, forgive the pun; that anything mystical or occult about their images should be taken simply as the taste for religious and feudal icons. Yet the Viéville exuded divining knowledge at every turn. Its pips, with their minute variations from one number to the next, implied specific outcomes, both failures and triumphs. And the several face cards whose mouths appeared to be erased into smoke, as if the artist wanted the wind to scatter them, could not help but warn of supernatural retaliation against careless speech.

There was one card in the Viéville that showed up inordinately in my three-card draws, so much so that I was convinced that it transmitted an especially urgent message. The twelfth major arcanum, Le Pendu, shows a man strung up by one foot. The other leg is gracefully bent at the knee, the ankle folded behind the straight leg. At first glance, Le Pendu seems to be upside-down, hanging from a gallows. Yet the roman numeral of this card, XII, is itself upside down and backward. In order to read that numeral in the "right way" the card must be rotated one hundred eighty degrees. Now, it is Le Pendu who is righted in an inverted world where the ground is above and the sky below. He looks to be levitating from his fastened foot. And his hands are all but concealed behind his back, his fingertips peeking out above his shoulders. For the arms to be twisted in such a way would certainly require dislocation, perhaps even tearing of muscle and ligaments. But if I blurred the focus of my eyes just enough, those fingertips lost their precision and looked more like feathers, and Le Pendu's ambiguous facial expression tended toward a smile. So Le Pendu, rather than a victim of torture, became a magical bird capable of turning his suffering upside down into triumph.

That first day with the Viéville tarot I drew Le Pendu twice. And the day that my doctor asked me to consider a bone marrow transplant, I drew it again, along with two cards I can no longer remember. In my dreams that night, I drew three cards on purpose, upsetting the usual etiquette in which interpretation occurs after the card draw. I pulled the three cards that I somehow knew indicated the future, ectoplasmic and halting and yet certain: the Ace of Cups, the Devil, and the Pope. Upon awakening, I wrote down what I remembered from the dream: l'As de Coupes showed the New Jerusalem, no longer the bucolic heaven of Ancient Greece or the original garden of Eden, but rather a walled city, with edifices of gold and towers of silver, and diamonds and rubies for parapets and spires. The New Jerusalem was impregnable and self-reliant, and it was everything I was before the Eddans, and that which I hoped to become once more.

The Viéville version of Arcana XV, Le Diable, was different from depictions in other Marseille tarots. He is usually a horned beast slave-driver, holding two naked souls. But in the Viéville, he is alone, striding to the left, in profile, his head a combination of bearded man and winged, fire-breathing dragon. His shoulder, stomach, and knees all bear human faces. His red tail is in the form of an 'S.' In my dream, he seemed to be looking menacingly at the New Jerusalem, as if he were about to storm it.

Arcana V, Le Pape, is seated with his halved-hat, his miter, and his right hand, fingers folded into a blessing. He is looking down and toward the right, sorrowfully perhaps, his perfectly aquiline nose above a voluminous beard of Old Testament proportions. Two cardinals look up at him, entreating him for some favor. But his decision is not for either of them, for he is looking far toward the right field, into the future.

I drew these cards because until that moment, I had believed that I had led a good life. But, no, that was an untruth. I had led an easy life, a life barricaded, like the Ace of Cups, against want, a life in which it had been too easy to be good. The little cross I had to bear was my health, and, until that point, it had been a cross that was easy to carry. At the very moment that my health was now in trouble, I was also troubled by insistent thoughts I did not recognize. What would it be like to tear down someone else's Jerusalem? This was the question I pondered as I sat at my table that morning, mulling over the previous night's dream and my apparently new ability to control my actions during a dream. I had only one lingering doubt, and I resolved to put it to rest through one final visit to Augustine.

$$\bigcirc \quad \bigcirc \quad \bigcirc$$

It was dark this time, very late at night or very early in the morning. He was sitting on his cot, yawning as if he had only just awakened, but his gestures were brisker than I had remembered. He was attaching the strap on one of his sandals when he froze, suddenly aware of my presence. He looked up slowly, squinted to assure himself that it was indeed I. Then, he sighed.

"You're here early this time."

"Forgive me, yes. I could come back another time if it helps."

"No, it's no bother. I was only going to Matins. I am happy to stay and visit with you." He unfastened the sandal strap. "What is it on your mind?"

He frowned and peered at me, though it was so dark that he could not have seen much on my face. Then, again, I don't know what he ever could have seen on my bird's face. What expression could be transmitted there, and would it be something that humans could decipher?

"Father, there is something that I have always wondered about you. I am only now asking you, but this has troubled me for some time, long before you and I ever met. What it is . . . ," I stalled, and then finally blurted out, " . . . is that you believe in demons."

He must have been expecting something else, because his face dropped. After some moments, he said, "Annika, you know that I am a loyal servant of God . . . "

"That's not what I meant. I don't say that you worship demons, only that you believe in their existence."

Now he frowned, as if I were spouting gibberish. "Of course. Demons exist."

"Father, in my land, it is not something we take for granted."

"I don't understand."

"Belief means something different to the people in my land. Most people, including those who believe in Jesus Christ, also believe in science ... in observing the natural world. We are a civilization that depends on science for all aspects of survival. And science has discounted the presence of demons and ghosts and spirits. So even those Catholics who are sincere in their belief would tend to say that demons are a vestige of an earlier time, before science disproved the existence of all such superstitious ideas."

Augustine frowned and gazed downward, genuinely grappling with my words. But his kindly manner returned after a few moments, and he genuinely seemed relieved. After swallowing and pausing, he resumed. "I can see that, for an outsider, the distinction between belief in demons and worship of demons might be blurry, but you know me well enough to know that these are entirely separate. I do not worship thieves, but I would be a fool if I denied their existence. As for whether the existence of demons can be verified by your ... science ... ask yourself the following: would your gut, your intuition, your soul not be well positioned to ascertain or deny such beings?"

"That's just it, Father. Science teaches that observation and verification must come from outside the subject. You can't go by your gut to prove or deny anything. Others need to be able to experience it, too. It needs to be duplicable, verifiable, measurable."

"But we have only to turn to Genesis to see the earliest verification of the greatest of demons ... "

"Again, that is not verifiable. Some believers in my land say that the story of Adam and Eve in the Garden of Eden is just that, a story. An allegory for true phenomena like temptation and the choice between good and evil, but a story nonetheless."

"I see. And what about the Gospels? Are they also merely stories?"

"No, Father. Believers regard those as truth."

"Very good. So what do you make of the statement that Christ cast out the demons from the Magdalene? Or, when Christ himself went into the desert, and was tempted, by the devil or Satan, depending on the Gospel? Were those also mere allegory?"

"Father, these events may well have happened. But what the Evangelists called 'the devil' and 'Satan,' could these in fact be elements of human sinfulness? Why ascribe to them outside reality, when we find all the evidence of the existence of evil within humans?"

"Hmm . . . ," he said thoughtfully, with a smile. "You remind me of how I was as a young man, before I met Ambrose. I was always trying to prove that I was right, that others weren't nearly so clever. And then Ambrose told me of Anthony of the Desert, and how he struggled against demons. You see, I always knew that demons exist. Everyone around here knows that, for the desert is not far away, and the desert is full of spirits. Now, my resplendent *malayka*, you are one of them, you know? You are a spirit from the desert, perhaps not from the desert I know, but your land sounds impoverished and dry in its own manner, so a desert just the same. It's odd that you would doubt the existence of your own kind."

"I am not a demon!"

"You are not an evil spirit, but you are not far from becoming one. I think that you are an errant angel. Perhaps you will be forgiven and saved . . . "

"You sound like Origen now. You attacked him for believing in the possibility of salvation for Satan and demons, and yet you entertain the same possibility for a demon like me!"

Augustine darkened and glowered at me. I walked outside his cell just as the sky was lightening in the east. I stayed there for some time, not knowing whether he was so disgusted with me as to refuse my company. But I heard his door creak open, and he beckoned for me to walk with him. We descended the hill on the dusty road that was surrounded by almond trees and vineyards, the fragrance of sage and the sea periodically wafting around us. Without once looking at me, he began to speak: "My dear *malayka*, it sounds like the manners of your people are such that God's presence is minimized at every turn. Your kind says that He does not exist, that He has forgotten us, that He should not let evil things occur. And now, from what you are telling me, it sounds like your people are also saying that our need for His help in resisting temptation is not nearly as acute as we think it to be. For if demons do not exist and we ourselves are the source of all evil, then we could also be the source of all good. One less reason to believe in Him.

"You also accuse me of Manichaeism by saying that my belief in the existence of demons necessarily entails a belief in the limits of God's power. If demons exist, then we have a dualistic universe in which the power of God does not always triumph over the power of Satan.

"You yourself, my beloved *malayka*, seem to have somewhat of a theological formation. So you must surely know that God has given to humans the great gift of free will. He allows us to choose between good and evil. There are any number of demons ready to draw us into sin. If God destroyed those demons, and if he withdrew our free will, we would all be united in Christ. But God so values the *choice* to love him, not only love but the choice of love, that he permits spirits and demons to persist.

"We may not like His decision. We may cry out to God that the demons threaten us at every turn. And He hears us when we cry out. That is what prayer is.

"But make no mistake, *malayka*. Demons do exist, and God permits them to exist because they can make us firmer in our faith, in our resolve, in our belief. So, without their intending to do so, they are furthering God's work.

"You come from a place that is overly attached to empirical truth. So I will give you an example from your own life, that you may have first-hand proof that demons are among us. You have spoken to me of your great sadness and fear early in the morning, when you first awaken. You have said that your thoughts vary, that you could be worrying about family, your vocational duties, or your health, but that whatever the subject, you inevitably worry. And you have described the sensation of this worry as it apprehends you. One moment, you are sleeping soundly, confident and at peace. The next moment, you feel assailed, as if something sitting at the foot of your bed has been waiting for you to open your eyes so that it can pounce.

"That, dear *malayka*, is your demon. He does not bother with appearance. His form would make him laughable, so he hides in invisibility, behind a wall of recrimination. He has studied you for years, and he knows that you are weakest when you feel that you have failed in your responsibilities. He wants you to lose faith in God. And perhaps you already have, although I dare to hope that, if you are here with me, it is because you want to believe in Christ. So he wants you to despair further, to lose all hope, to give up your responsibilities. And from the sound of things, he has nearly succeeded at all of this.

"If you wave away his existence as so many thoughts and failings of your own, you are further isolating yourself from God's mercy. For you are really telling yourself that your demon is merely a series of unpleasant thoughts to which you must accustom yourself. As if God would wish that on any of His children!

"I will tell you of my demon, *malayka*. For one has pursued me since I was a child. We all have guardian angels, and we may well all have personal demons, each one of us subject to a particular demon's attacks. I cannot speak for others, only for myself.

"She is the wind. Growing up in Thagaste, the wind is constantly present. Occasionally, it is a wind from the sea, cool and comforting, the kind of breeze that brings freshness to the vineyards in the afternoon. But that sort of wind is just a visitor. The one who lives here, who is the permanent owner, is the demon who has whispered to me my whole life. She is loudest when I have been alone. One afternoon when my mother put me down to nap with my nurse and her own children, I awoke even as everyone else slept. It was very hot. I sat up on the cot, and all was quiet, but then the wind breathed hot in my ears, and she told me of where she came from, a desert so large that it would take a camel train a month to cross it, only no camels could cross it except during the night, so merciless was the sun. 'You are on the edge of an ocean much vaster than that little sea of which you are so fond, pretty boy. Set your sights on the golden ocean instead. Come back with me.' I looked down and shook my head, and she left me alone for the rest of the day, but was back the next morning when I played with my mother's comb as I lay on the floor. She whispered to me of caravans traveling by the light of the stars, of her breathing on those riders, and of the occasional caravan occupant (it was normally a slave) who could not bear the endless sand and stars. Such battered souls could not travel by starlight and sleep during the day, even though the facts were plain; movement during the day was fatal. She tried to comfort the mad riders who were, fortunately, rare enough, but who always ended up the same. They would wait until sunrise for the caravan to set up camp, and then when all were in tents settling down to sleep, they would run, as fast and as far as possible, sometimes making a good distance, perhaps as far as a mile, before the sun dissipated whatever energy they had left, and they burned under the day star and died before noon. This demon, the wind who wanted me to follow her, whispered many such riders to death.

"'Let me speak to you, pretty boy. I know a thousand tales. You, who read too much to escape your boredom—I would make it so that you never knew boredom. Come with me.' Each time, I said 'no.' And each time, she would return the next day or week or month, each time with a more elaborate tale. As an adolescent, she would tempt me with carnal pleasure and total knowledge, a mastery not only of the texts I knew but had not yet read, but of texts hidden, obscure, even those not yet written."

By now, we had reached the top of a hill not far outside the gates of Hippo. I had not noticed where we had been walking, but instead was thinking of the golden ocean and riders running from their caravans. And there, suddenly, I was, overlooking the blue sea that was very fine, Augustine's demon's jealousy notwithstanding. He saw me stare at that color, to which I should by then have been accustomed. But that blue was never domesticated; it never let itself be remembered properly, but just faded into a newspaper-ink version of itself. Then, with each new sighting, it disarmed me again. "It is good of you to talk to me of these things, Father. I am grateful."

He smiled and nodded. It was the most relaxed, even congenial I had ever seen him.

"Will you answer one more question of mine, and then I promise that I'll leave you in peace?"

"I will do my best."

"Do you still disagree with Origen on the matter of final salvation for Satan and demons?"

"Naturally," he said with no hesitation, still smiling.

I turned back to the sea and said, "Then there is no hope of salvation for me."

His face clouded with confusion, and he shook his head and tried to prevaricate, but it was no use. He had momentarily forgotten that he believed me to be a demon, and was now going to the trouble of reconciling his dogma with the now irrefutable truth that he liked me, considered me in a friendly light, and certainly did not wish for me eternal damnation. I have, in the intervening years, come across mention of "morning demons," a concept supposedly discussed by some of the early Church Fathers. Morning demons were apparently not uncommon to those poor, malnourished, stinking, bearded men who lived on the outskirts of an empire that was no longer an empire, just a tattered cloth of ill-fitted strips. That day was the last time I ever visited Augustine in Hippo. I recall standing on that hilltop for some time at his side, feeling his unease after he stopped trying to hide the fact that he believed in the inevitability of my damnation. Augustine was a sincere friend to me. He would not have wanted me to suffer. And his speaking of my morning fear and guilt as a sort of demon was a grace that manifested itself only later, when I learned of the existence of other morning demons. Only then did I feel somewhat less alone in my suffering. I have always been unoriginal, even in my struggles with the occult.

Let me return to the topic of the beginning of this chapter: the desire to know what will happen. For I had turned from prognostic algorithms to tarot, and from tarot to Augustine, all in the hope of knowing how much time was left to me, and what will happen after I die. Undergirding this conversation and my many tarot excursions was a feeling of guilt, for all manner of divination and fortunetelling are expressly forbidden by the Church. The Catechism describes these activities as means of seeking mastery, over the future or even of God. They are violations of the First Commandment because they substitute something else, for instance, knowledge of power, where God should be as the central preoccupation of our lives. So, to the extent that I believed in tarot's predictive powers more than God's mercy and providence, I sinned. But I was always ambivalent about this subject. I was afraid that I was concocting justifications for my use of tarot, but I nevertheless credited tarot, particularly Le Diable, with making possible that last talk with Augustine. And in that last conversation, Augustine planted seeds of mercy in the form of little morning demons, caught red-handed and finally exposed as the thieves they really are. I pursued an illicit practice, and God nonetheless triumphed as a result of it. Perhaps salvation was possible for a morning demon like me.

CHAPTER TEN
His Last Confession[*]

IT WAS MONTHS BEFORE I AGAIN SAW THE *malayka*. In the meantime, I settled into my new life as an imprisoned exile, trapped within the walls of Hippo during the Vandals' siege. Those were days of great tribulation, with there never being enough food, and the fields and orchards that fed Rome for hundreds of years inaccessible, just beyond the gates. We watched as men with sun-colored hair tore down fruit trees, gorging themselves on olives and apricots. They spoke a rough language unlike Latin or Greek, and all of them had wrinkles at the corners of their eyes, as if they were used to squinting at long distances. Disease ran rampant as those sun-haired men stacked corpses of slaughtered peasants outside the walls of the city. Yet we would also see groups of them assembled in a circle, with a priest chanting and praying and distributing the Holy Eucharist. What manner of Christian could keep the Sabbath, yet spend the other six days of the week cutting down his fellow Christians? But we held firm, keeping the enemy at bay as they ravaged much of the rest of the North African coast, from Mauretania Caesariensis to Numidia and Tripolitania. My own part to play was accidental, as I was in Hippo only because Augustine had the grace to welcome me after the Vandals had taken over my own village of Calama. Clergy were given the choice of either converting to the Arian

---

[*] Editor's note: see the Editor's note for Chapter Four.

heresy, or else exile or execution. May God be praised that Augustine made it so that I should not be put to that test! Once safely arrived in Hippo, I accustomed myself to a maddening regularity. I rose every morning and prayed and sang with the brothers. I then said Mass in a chapel in town, where attendees included widows and mothers, farmers and fishermen, merchants and beggars. When able, I helped our physician, the one who administered to Augustine in his last days, with cases that required little medical expertise. And thus I learned a bit of the medical arts, in ministering to those who suffered from coughs, dropsy, bad teeth, bad hearing, and bad digestion. I treated animals, too: heifers outraged that they could not leave the city to graze, disconsolate poultry, skittish horses. Most importantly, I listened to and heard confession from Hippo's terrorized inhabitants, the newly arrived refugees from Rome, the recently enfranchised slaves who now looked for work, and the farmers caught, like me, inside city walls.

In retrospect, the siege was much kinder than the ensuing conflagration. After giving every indication that he had given up on Hippo, King Geiseric returned in full force to breach our walls and set the city aflame. While the siege was a time of suffering, there were plenty of opportunities to reflect on the past. Such a luxury vanished the moment that Geiseric began to single out the nobles and clergy. In those last days where free thought was still occasionally possible, I ruminated over what Augustine said to me the last time we spoke. He was lying in his cot, propped up with blankets and cushions looking at the penitential psalms he had asked one of the brothers to copy and affix to the wall in front of him. *So that I might better prepare for death*, he said. His breath was a mere rattle. He had lost what little flesh was still clinging to his bones, and his head was skull-like, his chin and cheekbones unusually protuberant. He had lingered on like this for a week, refusing visits from all but his physician and those who brought him his meals. (I insisted on this latter privilege whenever possible, so that I might see my friend, if only for a moment, before he returned to solitary prayer.) During this last conversation, he began feebly, the way that those near to death are wont to do, commenting on the sunshine and heat. He said how much he was looking forward to seeing his mother again. And then, quite unexpectedly, he somehow composed himself sufficiently to call out, in what would almost be considered a loud voice, "Grace is like honey that slowly pours over cracks in a jar. And my life began as the most bitter rejection of Our Lord. I tried my hardest to ignore Him. But grace filled in my cracks, and repaired my brokenness, and sweetened my bitterness."

I nodded and smiled in silence, for fear that I'd rob him of the chance to speak once more. He continued, "God in His grace has helped me to evade the demons that have stalked me. Although I began my life through a series of stumbles, his call to me gradually broke through the din of those demons. Praise be to God!"

I echoed his exclamation, and then watched as his face lost its brilliance, his voice its strength. He seemed at once to crumble.

"And in my book, I wrote on this: that the cleverest demons can sometimes masquerade as angels of light." He chewed his lip, inhaled jerkily, and continued, "I rebuked her in the beginning, but then I wanted to believe her. And now, I fear that I was duped by a demon after all."

He trailed off, and then asked me to leave so that he could return to prayer. And I could do nothing else but enter the monastery's library where Augustine's writings were housed, to look up the passage whose contents I had guessed, to make sense of what I already knew had been his last words to me:

The demons . . . [mislead] human beings by their subtle cleverness, either by breathing a secret poison into their hearts, or even by appearing to them in the deceptive guise of friends, making a few of them disciples of their own, and teachers of very many others. For it would be impossible for men to discover, without previous instruction from the demons themselves, the different likes and aversions of the various demons, the names by which they are to be invoked or compelled to do man's will. Hence comes the first appearance of the magic arts and their practitioners. But their most effective hold upon the hearts of mortals (and it is in the possession of them that they especially glory) is gained when they transform themselves into angels of light.

I didn't need to consult this text to know the obvious, that Augustine was of course referring to the *malayka*, the creature whom he had initially distrusted, but who had subsequently become his confidant. And the same *malayka* then came to me, seeking my advice, of all things! This in itself was already bad enough, and it was all I could do to keep my composure over the ensuing day and night, awaiting the inevitable news that His Holiness had passed on to his final reward, knowing that his soul fell victim to the trickery of the *malayka*. But after the funeral, as the contemptible routine of the siege set in, I thought even more about Augustine's last confession. Was it not strange, I thought, that His Holiness argued against the Manichaeans and their misguided belief in the powers of darkness? If Augustine indeed rejected the beliefs of his errant youth,* the belief that evil demons could prevail over God, that we all were subject to those demons' seductions, then why did he continue to believe in demons? By mentioning things such as demons and magic arts and their practitioners, wasn't Augustine implicitly admitting their

---

* Editor's note: Augustine was a Manichaean in his early adult years.

power? Was that not in itself blasphemous? And who was finally responsible for Augustine's lapse, if it was indeed a lapse: the *malayka*, or Augustine himself?

All these noxious doubts dogged me for months. I missed him no less. In fact, I mourned him with a despondency that was hardly fitting. I should have been glad to see my friend escape Hippo and the world that we knew was coming to an end. I should have rejoiced at the thought that he was now with Our Lord and Our Holy Mother. Instead, I worried for his soul. And the sting of mourning did not lessen with time, but hurt me with renewed force each time I awakened. The siege went on, and my doubts besieged me with no less persistence.

Then, the day of the breach came. For a few months prior, we had momentarily approached a state verging on happiness, having come to believe that we had worn down Geiseric, that he had run out of supplies, that he had perhaps run out of interest in our city, that he would focus his energies on Carthage instead. He left us alone for nearly two months, and our farmers began to sneak out before daybreak, initially on foot and then with their wagons, to reclaim fields that had been ravished and then neglected for so long. At the end of their expeditions, they brought back crops that had been commonplace before the war, but had since become impossible delicacies: apricots and olives, almonds, even honey, for the bees had never stopped their industrious maintenance of their hives. Our Lord was kind to us, and, after a few weeks of replanting, wheat began to trickle in for milling, so we could eat bread again. Then one morning, as our emboldened farmers opened the gates long enough for several wagons to pass through, a dozen sun-haired men appeared, probably having hidden in wait in ditches recently abandoned after the siege. They forced the gates wide open, commandeered some of the wagons, and drew swords on the farmers.

Our own sentinels were too late to react, and within a few minutes, a horn call summoned other soldiers on horseback.

Geiseric was calmer than I had imagined he would be. His hair and beard were long and neatly braided. His gestures were controlled, with the poise of a senator rather than a soldier. His accent was thick, but he spoke Latin well, and softly. He seldom had occasion to raise his voice. He was much taller than any North African. His eyes were also accustomed to squinting, as much to gauge the weaknesses of a fortress or man as the distance his army would need to travel in a day. And while I held no illusions as to his capacity to kill at any moment, I nevertheless saw a weariness toward killing and marching. This weariness was evident from the moment he entered the city gates, but I had ample opportunity to study it in detail. For, after setting fires and subduing any men who had tried to fight the Vandals, Geiseric's next order was to round up all the brothers of the monastery. He had us put in the monastery barn, where we stood amid sheep and pigs until fatigue forced us to sit and lie down in the straw and filth. We were locked up like this for a day, with nothing to eat but the food that we had happened to leave in the trough that morning. Guards prevented the townspeople from comforting us, although one was permitted to leave us a pail of water. That night, well after we would normally have retired, a guard asked for me, and grasped me unceremoniously by the shoulder as he steered me toward a house that had been transformed into Geiseric's quarters. Servants had barely started unpacking maps and belongings, which they had spread out on the dirt floor in no discernible order. A sleep roll in the corner was the only indication that Geiseric would set up his household in the space. Geiseric was sitting on the floor with his legs crossed. When he looked up, he blinked until his eyes could focus on me. There was only one small oil lamp near where he had spread out his map, and I thought that I recognized the coastline of Numidia, but I wasn't certain. Geiseric must have seen my searching glance, for as he stood up, he said, "Your mapmakers are good. They indicate sandbars and submerged rocks in the sea. Very helpful."

I remained silent.

"I hear that Augustine passed away. I want to convey to you my condolences."

"Thank you, my lord. His Holiness passed almost two years ago."

"Was it that long ago? Of course, you must be right. I have just lost track of time."

He looked back down at his map as he said, "You know, of course, why I have called you here."

I nodded, and said, "We will not renounce the True Faith, my lord."

He frowned, and then smiled, saying, "Ah, I see. You thought that I was going to make you a conversion speech." He even laughed a little. "No, there is no time to argue over one or three persons, over whether Christ was made or begotten, as your people say. No, you will be exiled from Hippo. There is no room for discussion on this. I was referring to the woman we picked up several days ago. I assumed that you knew about her. For she knows about you." He called out to one of his guards in his Vandal language, and in a few moments, another guard led in a veiled figure.

"We would never have noticed her, were it not for the fact that she speaks our language. She looks like your women. But she talks like ours. Imagine that, a Vandal woman here before any of us arrived!" And he laughed even more. The guard led the person in front of me, and she put down her veil, and even before she let down her veil, I could see the *malayka*'s plumage and wings. I sputtered and cried, "So you can see her too?"

153

Geiseric responded, "Why would I not be able to see her?" It dawned on me that what Geiseric saw was not what I saw. He referred to her as a woman, a woman who looked like other women in our land. No feathers or wings, no beak and nervous eyes, just a woman. I resolved not to say anything further, for fear of revealing too much.

"Repeat what you said to me to this priest." Geiseric's reasoned tone had vanished. The *malayka* darted her bird eyes around anxiously as she flapped her wings a bit. I wondered what Geiseric saw in the place of these bird gestures. She looked at me as she said, "I am about to do something horrible. And I need Father Possidius to tell me whether I am being afflicted by demons, or whether it is my own doing."

Geiseric looked at me expectantly, as if I would understand the *malayka*'s words in Latin more than he did. I remained silent. He said something to her in Vandal, and she responded in kind, and I wondered briefly if she were not all this time simply a Vandal spy. Then I grew furious with myself for overlooking the obvious, that she was neither Vandal nor Roman, but some sort of demonic creature who could assume bird and human forms. He said something to his guard, who led the *malayka* by the shoulder out of the room.

"How do you explain this?" Although Geiseric's voice had not changed in volume, his polite manner had vanished.

"My lord, I cannot explain it."

"Do you know the woman?"

"Well, yes . . . in that, I have spoken with her before. I do not know her."

Geiseric's eyebrows lifted as I stuttered. His lip curled, and he said, "Is she your whore? That is not allowed for you clerics, is it?"

"No, my lord," I said firmly. "Nothing unseemly has happened. I have spoken to her because she . . . used to visit His Holiness. He was her confessor." I did not know whether this was precisely true, for His Holiness had never mentioned administering the Rite of Reconciliation to the *malayka*. Nevertheless, it seemed close enough to the truth to convey the intention behind her visits.

"So she was Augustine's whore?"

"No, my lord, nothing of the kind. They only discussed things."

"What did they discuss?"

"I cannot say, my lord."

"You will say, or I will have the throat of one of your brothers cut." He sat back down to study his maps, and spoke his threat almost absently.

I pray God that He might forgive me for what I next said. For I said it in order to save the lives of my brethren, and perhaps my own miserable life. "My lord, she is a demon. We did not know this at first. His Holiness felt that she had duped him into believing that she was something else, a *malayka* . . ."

"What does that word mean?," he interrupted.

"*Malayka* . . . it is like an angel. But angels in our land are different. They can have wings. They are good; let's leave it at that. They are innocent."

Without warning, he stood again, strode right in front of me such that his chin almost touched my forehead (so much taller than me he was), and said quietly, "So she is a demon or witch, and she tricked you, and she is not one of you."

"That is right."

"So she is not a spy, and it makes no difference to you what happens to her."

"I do not wish her ill, but we are afraid of her. My lord, if I may ask, what do you see when you look at her?"

"What do you mean?"

"Do you see a woman, or something else?"

"What manner of stupidity is this? You are trying my patience, priest."

155

"Forgive me, my lord, but that is just it. When I look at her, and all the times that His Holiness looked at her, we saw a bird. She has the ability to hide her true appearance, and she seems to have done that with you. But please believe me, my lord, that she is not a woman."

Geiseric spat and stormed away, speaking a litany of presumably offensive words in his native language. He accosted his guard, took the man's sword, and barked an order for another guard to bring back the *malayka*, for she and her captor had been waiting just outside the door. Geiseric approached the *malayka* from behind, took the sword and pulled back her forehead, and slit her throat. She looked upwards as she beat her wings wildly and blood poured out of her neck, but she made no sound. I screamed, and Geiseric, who was watching me carefully, said, "You act strangely for someone who is watching a demon die."

And as much as I wanted to shout at him and curse him and run to comfort the *malayka*, perhaps offer her Last Rites and pray for her soul, I thought at the same moment that he was right. Why would I mourn a demon that had tricked my master and friend?

Geiseric had me thrown back into the barn, and I hid in a corner and said little to my brethren, certainly nothing about the *malayka*, for no one else had seen or heard me speak of her. The sun rose a few hours later, and I prayed with my brothers as we awaited word of Geiseric's order for our execution (for I was then convinced that he would have us killed as he had done with the *malayka*). There was nothing to do but pray and sleep, and I kept watch with my brothers as long as I could, until night again fell.

She visited me late that night. As I write this, I realize that this sounds like the ravings of a mad man. I did not dream her. I had been asleep, yes, but her presence awakened me. She was still alive, with a great, dark red slash at her throat, but otherwise no different than

156

before. I was lying on the ground, hugging my knees like a child. And she was at once there, also on the floor on her side, peering at me so closely, her beak touching my nose.

"I am about to do something horrible," she whispered, almost hissing through her beak.

I looked at her in terror, unable to speak at first. Then, I finally sputtered, "How are you here before me?"

She looked at me blankly, and repeated, "I am about to do something horrible. I would visit His Holiness, only he is no longer in this world. So I come to you."

"But you are dead!"

She stared at me as if I was out of my mind. Her plumage, which used to be iridescent, had changed into a uniform dark blue, nearly indistinguishable from the darkness of the barn. Her eyes were just as wild as when Geiseric had her killed, yet she genuinely seemed to have no recollection of that moment. "Please help me," she said again and again, and moved her wing to rest on my shoulder. Some of the brothers came over and tried to soothe me. They did not see her, and fortunately, did not seem to have heard what I said to her.

What I write next will most certainly seem fabricated. I wonder myself whether I did not dream this. But I must testify to what it is that I saw. I gave my brothers reason to believe that they had succeeded in calming me, and they dispersed. I sat up, and the *malayka* did too, and then she asked me to stretch out my legs and gently grasped my feet with her claws. I wondered that they did not rip my skin. And she suddenly bounded upwards, and I with her, upside down and suspended by my feet, and we flew in the night with stars but no moon to show the way. She did not fly far, although it seemed like an eternity. I was certain that she was going to drop me from a great height. But instead she angled toward a hill outside the city gates, gray in the starlight and cool with the breeze from the sea. She descended swiftly, but then slowed and hovered and beat her wings rapidly so that my fingers and hands gently touched the grass. She continued like this until all of my body was gently deposed onto the ground. I was breathless, gasping, and mortified, for my robe had fallen over my face and I was all but indecent. The *malayka* landed a few feet from me and contemplated me with some sternness, until I realized that she was not looking at me at all, but rather a figure behind me, with feet and hands bound and sitting up against a tree trunk. I sensed that it was Geiseric, but peered at him to be certain. He was also gagged and made no sound, but his eyes were hard with fear.

"Possidius, I have brought you here to be my judge. For I am contemplating a wicked act, and I need you to tell me whether I am under the persuasion of a demon, or am myself responsible." That much, she said softly and with kindness in her eyes. Then, she looked to Geiseric, and her voice changed, and the softness left her eyes. "He thought to make me suffer."

Daring at last to speak, I said, "He thought you were a demon. Either a demon, or a spy for us."

"No such thing. He used me, and disposed of me when he had no further use for me."

"*Malayka*, you are raving!"

"No, Possidius, I understand you clearly. For you see in this man a Barbarian raider, someone who besieged your town and will destroy your empire. And that's what raiders do. And if that is all that he did, then I wouldn't have paid him any mind. He could have sacked Rome, enslaved all its people, even slit my throat, and I wouldn't have borne him any ill will. That's what raiders do. It is in the natural order of things." She paused to breathe, and continued, "But what you see is not his true reality, Possidius. Just as he does not see me as

I truly am, you do not see him as he truly is. He is working to bring down my empire. I thought that he and I were working towards a common goal, not of bringing down that empire, but of strengthening it, renewing it. And I trusted him, befriended him, even. And then he sold me out, and then I knew that he was playing me, all along, playing on my weaknesses, playing on my deficiencies, my absences, the failures in my life. So while a raider is supposed to do all of this, a friend and colleague is not. That, Possidius, is why I am going to do this horrible thing."

Geiseric was motionless, but his eyes never left those of the *malayka*. I said nothing for some time, and then ventured, "What are you planning on doing to him?"

"I will destroy him."

"Then why don't you simply kill him?"

"You mean, the raider? There's no need to kill a raider. He will do what he is supposed to do. No, I will tear down the man you cannot see, the one who was supposed to be my colleague and friend. I will take from him what he took from me."

By this point, I had given up on any hope of seeing the sunrise, let alone living another day. Somehow, I dared to say, "Then His Holiness was indeed right, and you are a demon."

"What do you mean?" There was panic in her voice.

"Augustine, just before he died, told me that he suspected that you were a demon, after all. Not a woman, not a *malayka*, but a demon who had tricked him into thinking that you were an angel."

"I am no demon . . . ," she seemed to grasp for words, " . . . but I think that I am besieged by a demon. Afflicted by a demon. Because I am a good person, and never before would I have thought to destroy someone. That is why I have come to you, Possidius: to ask you whether I am in control of my actions, or whether a demon is driving me to do this?"

I felt exhilarated, ecstatic, for I was sure that she would next seize me with her claws and rip out my throat, or fly up with me into the sky and drop me down onto the jagged hilltop. It no longer mattered to me, for I was exorcising the demon that had entrapped my dear friend and master. "You are a demon, and you have fooled us all. We thought that you were some sort of *malayka*, an angel too young to be accepted back into heaven. We thought that you had work to do, either for your own kind or for ours. We thought that you were doing the will of Our Lord, and that you lived with the blessing of Our Lady. But you are none of these things. You are Annika, an afflicted demon who is convinced that someone has done you wrong, and you will exact vengeance. That is what a demon does. I can say no more."

The *malayka* (and I realize the irony, that I have not ceased to refer to her as a *malayka*. But how strange it is to change the name of someone we have known, even if only for a short time!) looked at me with great suffering, but she did not strike out as I had expected. She flapped her wings a little, enough to hop over to where Geiseric was bound, and with her wingtip, forced open his mouth, and then breathed into his mouth with her beak. This took only a moment, and then she backed off from him, and looked at me once more with unspeakable pain. Then, she crouched down, sprang up, and flew into the night.

It took me a few moments to come to my senses. I ran over to Geiseric, and with clumsy fingers, unbound his hands and feet, and released him from the tree. I took off the gag, and he spit and wretched for a moment, but said nothing. Then, I waited. And this proved a long time, for Geiseric rubbed his hands and feet to regain circulation, and then sat up and peered at the night sky, eventually brightening in the east. He said nothing, and did nothing other than stare. After what I imagine was an hour, he stood up, perhaps confident in the growing daylight that he would be able to spot the *malayka* if she returned. He gestured toward me, grasped me by the shoulder, and roughly led me down the hill and toward the gates of Hippo. We walked through with little fanfare, and Geiseric forced me back into the barn, never once saying a word to me. That was the last time I saw him. And while I expected death at any moment, all I received was notice from one of his soldiers that my brothers and I were banished forever from Hippo, and that we had only a few days to flee to Roman-controlled territory, or else we would be killed as heretics. And we fled, and somehow made it to a safer place, and to this day, cling to life in a world that is ever more hostile to Our Lord and his priests.

His Holiness was right, all along. There are demons everywhere, living in the hills, the sea, the rivers, in villages and towns and even the great city of Rome, all looking to turn us away from God. And there are demons within us, too, skulking where we believe the fortress of our soul to be impregnable.

○

CHAPTER ELEVEN
My False Confessions

THE BASEMENT WAS COVERED WITH A dark blue synthetic low pile carpet, with intermittent, pea-sized, beige spots that could have been mistaken for stains, but were only part of the design pattern. The carpet did a good job of dampening noise, though. It was installed by plant managers who anticipated traffic from carts, the cumbersome audio-visual towers-on-casters that transported stacked VCRs, DVD/CD players, and television screens between classrooms. The carpet was installed back when the building was first renovated, in 1997. Ten years later, new plant managers again overhauled the building. The edifice I'm describing was the university library, built in 1980. At that time, the basement was just one large, book-bearing floor among others; it contained no rooms or dividing walls. After the 1997 renovation, the basement was partitioned into four classrooms, two on either side of a corridor covered with the aforementioned blue-and-beige carpet. The classrooms were intended to serve as occasional workspaces for groups of students visiting the library for a research project. Then the 2007 overhaul came, and the mobile A/V carts that used to be shared among faculty using those four classrooms were replaced with stereo cabinets (DVD/CD players, but also cables for projecting from a laptop computer to a large in-class screen) built into each classroom, such that no professor went without A/V equipment while teaching.

That I can talk now of a basement that was sectioned into rooms and a walkway may seem unremarkable, only those rooms and that walkway owe their very existence to a decision that reveals much about the priorities of the American university at the turn of the twenty-first century. For our senior administration had voted in 1996 to divest the library of its books. The chancellor's office explained to us that books were a poor investment of money and space. Digital collections were regarded as the logical next step in collection management. And so the University of X was compelled not only to cease purchasing new hard copies of books and journals and magazines, but also to find places to store its existing collections. "Store" is too polite a word for what this really entailed, a scheduled banishment to an "off-campus location" (we never found out where) for all books and volumes that had sat, unchecked out, for a minimum of a year. Naive administrators, solicited for their approval of this measure, imagined that only the "bad" books would be relocated through this arrangement, with "bad" meaning boring or outdated. But the truth, of course, was that the vast majority of the library's books had not been checked out for over a year. With the measure passing unanimously, the way was clear to empty whole floors that had previously housed bookshelves and little else. And thus, the granite-floored basement, suddenly emptied of its heavy load, could welcome its first carpet, a furnishing that, in 1997, had been a symbol of fresh ideas and re-purposing but that had, by the most recent renovation in 2017, become embarrassingly archaic. For that rug, with its color and texture, clashed with the monochromatic "smart classrooms" that replaced the stupid (for how else could they be described?) classrooms that had been there before. Smart classrooms were miniature versions of the two-color steel and concrete skyscrapers that one could find in any city across the globe, from

Dubai to Shanghai to Houston, a cross between Frank Gehry and Ikea. I had never seen space at the University of X go unused; most classrooms were busy on a daily basis from eight in the morning until at least six in the evening. But these rooms were empty and unlit, since the motion sensors connected to the lights languished, never tripped. The only lighting came from the fluorescents that shone over the main corridor. The previously opaque walls were replaced with sheet glass from floor to ceiling. There were a few white conference tables on casters and twenty or so pivoting adjustable black chairs. The library was obliged to use the smart classrooms as promised, on an ad hoc basis, and so it could not rent out the space to other schools within the university. The resulting paradox was painful: amid a severe shortage of space, prime real estate went unused. It was there, in vacant, costly space where the university of the future was born and where the library of the past perished, that I recorded my video talks.

I still have the scripts. Here is the first one:

Dear members of the Eddan Collective! Welcome to my channel. I decided to communicate with you all by this means, for reasons that will become apparent shortly. Let me begin by thanking you all for collaborating on this project, of returning to Marx as a way forward, a way out from under the crippling inertia of our government and university's administration, as well as our spiritual wasting away. Your commitment to this project is humbling to me, and your contributions to our mission and strategic plan are invaluable.

I want to begin in what is perhaps a too obvious manner, by examining definitions for three of my favorite words: abjure, renounce, and forswear. Merriam-Webster's Collegiate Dictionary, 11th edition, defines "abjure" as "to renounce upon oath," and indicates both "renounce" and "forswear" as synonyms. But here is where it gets interesting. I'll quote Merriam-Webster directly:

ABJURE *implies a firm and final rejecting or abandoning often made under oath* <*abjured the errors of his former faith*>. RENOUNCE *often equals* ABJURE *but may carry the meaning of disclaim or disown* <*renounced abstract art and turned to portrait painting*>. FORSWEAR *may add to* ABJURE *an implication of perjury or betrayal* <*I cannot forswear my principles*>. (pg. 3)

That's quite a lot to ponder, isn't it? These three words, as it turns out, are pertinent to the Eddans, or at least to two of its co-founders: Syd Niall and me. Let me cut to the chase: I hereby <u>abjure</u> the Eddans, because under Syd's leadership, the group has <u>renounced</u> its own principles. I do not say this lightly. Let me explain.

I am abandoning the current goals of the Eddans because they are informed by Syd's specific research agenda. And that agenda is thoroughly regressive, for he seeks to normalize Capitalism by demonstrating that it is the logical culmination of a species' evolution. Give any creature enough time and ensure that it does not go extinct, and you will see that "survival of the fittest" invariably means a system whereby the strong own the means of production and the weak supply the labor. Don't just take my word for it: look up Syd's publications to see for yourself. If this is how the Eddans wish to proceed, count me out. But I have faith in you, the true Eddans, that you never intended such infidelity to Marx. So, if you stand with me, stay tuned for what could be our next steps.

But I cannot, must not stop here, with only a critique of Syd's leadership. For if his loss of faith in Marxism were the only issue, I would not bring my complaint to you. I would speak with him, privately, and we would work out our differences. Syd's misdeeds go much further. You see, Syd has forsworn his principles, not only those of the Eddans, but basic principles of right conduct in the workplace. He has embarked upon a romantic relationship with a fellow faculty member. While this is not strictly forbidden *according to the University of X's policy, it is frowned upon, and it makes matters worse that said faculty member is also a co-founder of the Eddans. But even this would be something one could overlook.*

What I cannot overlook, however, is that Syd has been violent toward me. A few weeks ago, he and I met with our Dean after the faculty meeting. We had a difference of opinion about the direction of the Eddans. After we left the Dean's office, our disagreement continued even as he invited me back to his apartment. While I at no point attacked or otherwise touched or infringed upon Syd's person, Syd punched my face several times. I have photos that show the injuries.

(With this, I held up three photographs I had taken of myself the day after our last conversation, photos I had taken of myself in my bathroom. They showed a black eye and swollen lips.)

I decided not to call the police, and I will not press charges. It is my sincere, heartfelt hope that Syd seeks treatment for his condition, for I do believe that it is a condition and not a character flaw that drove him to be abusive toward me. Nevertheless, this condition has impelled Syd to betray the trust I placed in him, that we all placed in him. Syd's research, it is true, saved perhaps thousands of lives in the recent earthquake. That is his work. But he undertakes projects, knowing full well that he does not believe in the projects' goals. And he is currently incapable of the basic restraint that we expect from administrators and leaders. Syd has forsworn the trust that you and I have placed in him. He has broken a confidence. And so, I abandon the project, but not the work. My next video will have to do with what we, you and I, can next accomplish.

I arrived at the end of my typed script, which I placed on the table in front of me. The video shows me next looking into the camera with a panicked expression.

Only then did I realize that I'd need to shut off the camera. But that expression was also due to my numbed awareness of what I was about to do, in making this video public. I was at the time a complete amateur at making videos, and I had no idea how to edit footage. Anyone with any sense would have deleted those last few seconds. Many of the viewer comments left under the video in the hours and days after I posted the speech remarked on that look of panic. They said that it proved that I was terrified, and thus that what I recounted was true. I must have been a victim of Syd's violence, for what else would explain my darting eyes and trembling lips?

I am getting ahead of myself. I somehow figured out how to upload the video from my camera to YouTube and sent an invitation to the entire Eddans mailing list. Within fifteen minutes, Leta called me, repeatedly, but I didn't answer and never listened to the two voicemail messages she left. Within twenty minutes of posting the speech, I began to receive a torrent of emails and text messages, which I never read. And by four o'clock that afternoon, YouTube sent me a take-down notice, referring to an ongoing criminal investigation. I was at home, and remained in bed even when there was knocking at the front door.

The events of the subsequent days are not clear. I recall only one thing: Syd never pressed charges, for defamation or slander or anything else. But he did file for a restraining order, which obliged us to avoid one another. The lack of charges did not go by unnoticed among the commentators for my first speech. Several of them wrote to the effect that Syd's silence communicated assent to my accusations. One morning, as I left my apartment to walk to work, I was accosted by a reporter and her camera man.

"Do you feel vindicated at Syd Niall's apparent decision not to contest your claims, Professor Trent?"

"No comment."

That was the easy part. But even as the dejected news pair stopped trying to catch up with my brisk step, another man who had been trailing us sped up to take their place.

"Professor Trent, my name is [. . . I never caught his name]. Are you currently seeking legal representation? My firm offers a variety of services . . . "

"No, thank you."

Undeterred, he continued, "Don't be so quick to refuse legal aid, Professor Trent. You are aware, aren't you, of the ramifications of your actions?"

I stopped and squinted at him. "What do you mean?"

His lip curled and he grew surly. "Surely you knew, Professor Trent, that you'd be leaving yourself open to any number of attacks from all sides. Professor Niall could decide at any time to file suit. Perhaps his lawyer is already preparing to do so. Just because he hasn't done so yet doesn't mean he won't do so in the future. And your employer, your co-workers in the Eddan group . . . ," and here his voice changed oddly, " . . . You are besieged by demons, Professor Trent."

I froze in my tracks and faced him directly, and he stopped talking and sighed, as if caught red-handed. And we just stood in silence, for perhaps a minute, and then he finally said, "We are everywhere, Annika. Your dear Augustine taught you that."

"Am I one of you?"

At that, the lawyer's face dropped in what seemed to be genuine perplexity. "No, Annika," he then said, laughing. "If you were, you'd know it without any doubt." With that, he shrugged as if to admit that the jig was up, and started to walk away. He half-turned to call out, "By the way, you really should get a lawyer."

And a few minutes later, I began to think that he was perhaps right, given the summons to the Dean's Office that was taped to my office door. He would see me at 10:00 a.m.; there was no room in that mandating tone for negotiation. I sat in the Dean's reception, keeping my eyes lowered, so that I would not cross the surreptitious glance of the Dean's secretary, who had until that day always been warm toward me. I felt her eyes search my face and limbs for bruises. But my arms were covered with long sleeves as usual, and the contusions on my cheeks had long since receded. The Dean's door opened, and he called out neutrally, "Come in, Annika," barely standing from his conference table. He sat back down, gesturing for me to take the seat opposite him.

He began, "Annika, I'm sure you know why I've called you in today."

"Yes, I imagine I do."

He had dark circles under his eyes, which were of indeterminate color. I frowned, realizing that I had remembered him incorrectly. He was supposed to be handsome in the manner of aging surfers who finally accede to the demands of adulthood, who get a proper haircut that better hides the transition of their dirty blond into silver, who never quite give up their grip on unearned beauty. He was supposed to be that, this veteran surfer turned bureaucrat, and yet now I saw that my imagination had imposed that guise onto him, for his large, dark, sad eyes could never be the eyes of someone who scanned the horizon for waves, just as his mottled hair, brown and black and gray with no particular pattern, would never have been the hair of someone who spent any time in the sun. In fact, he looked nothing like my previous memories of him. He was a sad man who passed his days locked up in fluorescent light. That was all.

Those eyes passed over me now as one more task to complete. He peered at me squarely, but that pained him, and his eyes lowered as he said, "Regardless of whatever you allege happened between you and Syd, what you did is unacceptable. If you are telling the truth, you should take your case to the police. And if you are lying, it is because you nurse some grudge against Syd; and no matter what you resent about him, character assassination is unjust." He paused, and then continued, "Do you have anything to say so far?"

I said nothing.

"I've decided to place you on paid leave for the semester. You have been removed from teaching, and you are expressly forbidden from meeting or interacting with the Eddans."

I scoffed, "You really think that you can prevent me from communicating with other faculty members?"

"Try me." He had stopped looking at his hands that were folded on the conference table and was looking at me now, the sadness replaced by hardness.

"I see that you haven't thought this through. So, let me help you. If you ever looked in my file, you'd have seen that I have a documented medical condition. And recently my doctor has recommended an arduous procedure that may be the only chance I have of living a normal lifespan. I am a victim of a violent attack by a coworker, and I espouse a pacifist political philosophy. And you, a cis white hetero male with research support from aerospace and pharma—you think that you can make me disappear? Try me, because all I have to do is call the *Los Angeles Times*, and . . ."

He vaguely moved his hand as if to dismiss my words. "It's predictable that you'd threaten me." And my stomach clenched as I foresaw the worst sort of tit-for-tat in store for us. My eyelids drooped and my lips stretched first into a smile and then further into some sort of grimace. I couldn't see myself, but I saw the Dean's eyes widen with disgust. He called my name, and I slid down onto the floor.

When I came to, my eyes blinked open and shut, and my mouth had stopped grimacing. Both of us, the Dean and I, were sitting comfortably on a dark rug laid on the ground. We were in the shade of an enormous oak tree that itself was in a meadow. It was sunny and warm. The sky was mostly blue with stray white clouds drifting across it. There was a steady, gentle breeze. Perhaps ten miles away, snowcapped mountains loomed. It was as tranquil a setting as anything I might have imagined. There were a ceramic pitcher and two cups, and plates full of figs and cheese. And there was the Dean, looking at me placidly, a hint of a smile on his lips. He gazed at me as I registered surprise at our surroundings. When I had sufficiently calmed down, he said, "We have both seen far too much to waste our time bickering. Shouldn't we just start over?"

"What does that mean, to start over?" My stupor of just a few moments ago wasn't completely gone, for I had trouble pronouncing my words. But I felt well enough to reach for a fig, and I sipped the delightfully cold water from the cup in front of me.

"Let me reintroduce myself, Annika. You have made it your life's work to study a dying empire. And I am the nurse in a convalescent home to another dying empire. So we have that in common."

After a few moments of chewing and swallowing a fig, I stumbled through another sentence: "There's no need for melodrama." It was hard to be angry when the fig tasted so delicious.

"This isn't melodrama. It's time for my particular empire to die. My job is to ensure that its passing is as painless as possible."

"What do you want, Constantine?" It was the first time I dared to call him by his real name.

He smiled, joyful to hear me call him that. "To begin with, I want to avoid a senseless legal battle with you. As I'm sure you do as well. So, if I let you continue to teach, are you going to stir up more trouble with Syd?"

"I don't know... depends on whether he wants to stir up trouble with me."

"Oh, he doesn't, trust me."

"You've spoken to him?"

"Of course. He doesn't deny your accusations."

"Of course he doesn't, because my accusations are true."

"Yes." He paused to reach for a fig. "And I also know that his attack was provoked." He bit into the fig, all the while peering at me.

"Surely you don't think me capable of beating up Syd."

"No, I surely don't." He now drank from his cup. "I don't think that your violence toward Syd was physical. But I know that you were violent just the same."

"You can't know that. You can't prove that."

"Perhaps I can't prove it, but I know Syd well enough to know that it would take something unconscionable to make him beat up an invalid woman. So, unless a third party forced him to do it, the only suspect is you, Annika."

I squinted to be able to see the peaks of the mountains in front of us. "Constantine," I said after a while, "what is this place?"

"We are in Pannonia, which in our day would be shared between Hungary and Austria. Lovely, isn't it? It is out-of-time right now, but if we were in time, there would be people here, either working the fields or tending to the forest."

"Why are we here?"

"That's funny. I thought that, by bringing you here, I'd have an easier conversation with you. It's been difficult to convey to you the delicacy of the current situation of the University of X. It is always difficult to make faculty appreciate the precariousness of their workplace. But I figured that I had an in with you. You love terminal cases, after all. Well, this is a terminal case. The university, that is. Just as places like Pannonia were in the latter days of the Empire."

I was beginning to experience a slow elation, despite every certainty that I shouldn't. Here I was, calling him by his first name as if he were some wayward lover now regained, and relaxing into the taste of the figs and the cold water, and the air smelled of fresh grass just as it did on those long walks I used to take around the Institute when I was a graduate student. And the appearance of Constantine, to which I had previously been indifferent, was now also newly pleasant. His large dark eyes, which has been lamps of fatigue and despair, were now unreasonably kind and soft, the eyes of a mother keeping sleepless watch over a sick child. Those eyes now regarded me with tenderness as he said, "Did he really hurt you so terribly?"

"When he hit me? Yes, it hurt."

"No, before. Whatever he did to provoke you to hurt him, that in turn made him beat you. It must have been bad, whatever it was." There was no condemnation in those vigil eyes of his.

"Syd didn't hurt me at all. I fell in love with him, and I sent myself away to be with him. Inside him." Constantine's eyes displayed no skepticism at what I was saying; he either hid his emotions very well, or knew more about me than he had let on. "And then, I tried to tell him that I understood him. What makes him tick, I suppose. Only I shouldn't have done that. It made him feel violated. He had every right. I shouldn't have said what I did."

The bed-vigil eyes held my gaze as he continued, "Then why did you make the video with the speech, Annika?"

I looked away and breathed a bit more heavily, but said nothing. He dropped his question and set his sights past me, at a wooded valley that gradually descended from our meadow.

"Are you a *malayka*?" I whispered.

He chuckled and lowered his eyes. "Your Punic needs work, Annika. *Malayka* is a female noun, meaning a female angel."

"But you are an angel. Or else a demon."

Now, he looked away. I contemplated his fine eyes and noble nose and lips, asking myself why I had never before noticed his beauty or kindness. He eventually began again, all the while looking past me at the valley. "You and I need to come to an understanding, Annika. And, if you could agree to drop this senseless vendetta against Syd, I could in turn agree to let you teach, and let you continue your role in the Eddans. That would go a long way toward serving my interests."

"I don't quite follow."

He took my hand with great tenderness and clasped it the way that priests do when comforting family members of the deceased. "I need for our kind, yours and mine, to disappear. Those of us who were foolish enough to fall in love when we were young, with literature and history and philosophy — we who did that are now leeches. We are hemorrhaging the university; we are hemorrhaging our communities. And we continue to sell a product that students don't need, convincing them to assume an unnecessary financial burden."

"I don't understand what this has to do with me."

"You don't need to understand. Just know that groups like the Eddans allow me to consolidate departments in a manner that maintains the values of research and academic integrity. Isn't that what we should want?"

"Of course. Only . . . ," and I tried to say more, but I couldn't stop marveling at those eyes of infinite mercy, that never for a moment gave me any reason to suspect duplicity or ulterior motives. Constantine, or, as he now told me to call him, Darren was the first man other than my father to hold my hand. I smiled at the distant mountains, at the hints of more forest just between two starkly rising peaks. My mind grew blunt. I lost the ability to talk. And Darren slowly helped me to stand up, and then we were back in his office, and he led me out the door, past the receptionist who looked askance at us, and he said goodbye, and his hair was now blond, and he was again the aging surfer who had no time for me.

I had never been truly angry before. Perhaps I had experienced fleeting frustration, but never the sort of rage that made me taste blood. So it was with some concern that I began to notice anger taking root in me, springing up where I least suspected it. It appeared in isolated instances at first. During a lecture, for instance, when a student asked an unobservant question, I'd reply with carefully restrained impatience, making clear that it was only through a martyr's self-denial that I refrained from responding in the manner the student deserved. When coworkers asked innocent questions of clarification, I'd answer in such a condescending way as to intimidate anyone in the room from saying anything further. Worst of all, I began to dream of getting angry, something quite foreign as my dreams had always been routine and anodyne. I'd dream of flying into rages against coworkers, family members, and finally strangers, all straw men for me to chastise with my wrath.

It was thus with a smoldering heart that I sat down to write my second speech to the Eddans:

Hello, fellow members of the Eddan Collective.

Thank you for your support of my first speech. It is more gratifying than I can say to know that you have listened to me, that you are not turning your backs on me.

Now, let's get down to business, the business of the Eddans.

A few days ago, I read an interview with an ex-employee of Facebook. As you might imagine, he was not brimming with enthusiasm for his former job. He spoke about the requirement of all employees to report their daily activities on an internal social media platform, a sort of Facebook for insiders. Already a horrible proposition, to have to report to colleagues, not only supervisors, what you do every day. Only, it was worse than that, because employees were also instructed to make all of their activities demonstrations of "striving toward excellence." Maintaining the status quo of the company was explicitly unacceptable, and employees who did not show consistent innovation and improvements to the functioning of Facebook were fired.

Here's the kicker: the employee's critique of this management principle was that Facebook is already a "mature platform." Sure, improvements continue to be made, but these are mostly quibbles, little widgets and novel features that really don't add anything to the user's experience.

Does this sound familiar? Aren't we all, at the University of X and across corporate and research enterprises around the world, aren't we all being constantly harangued into doing whatever it is that we do, better or faster or stronger? And doesn't this cult of improvement begin to sound as shrill and empty as the proclamations of love of King Lear's two elder daughters? And aren't we, the honest workers (honest not only because we do not lie about the work we perform, but also because we are honest about the limits of possible improvement in our respective "mature platforms") aren't we therefore in the role of Cordelia, compelled by our integrity into saying, "Nothing, my lord" when our bosses ask us what we have to add?

The University of X and many other colleges and universities across the US are "mature platforms." Sure, research continues, but teaching methods for established disciplines are constantly being developed and revised, as if the underlying content of calculus or English literature or art history were radically changed every few years. Please note that I am not attacking or defending the existence of canons. Rather, I am observing that any of us, once we have displayed proficiency and mastery of our domain, must continue to speak the shibboleths of improvement. Admitting to doing the same task in the same manner, even if it is a task done well, is grounds for sanction, demotion, and even dismissal.

Marx had something interesting to say about this. As we all know, Marx wrote about the declining rate of profit, the inexorable drive toward zero profit that is the reason for Capitalism's insatiability. Without external stimuli, any enterprise's profits, no matter how robust initially, will diminish. And without increasing or at least stable profits, there would be no reason to invest in a business. This law is a cruel law, but capitalists regard it as the thing that spurs innovation and goads us toward greater productivity. The same law is also found in the physical world, the so-called Third Law of Thermodynamics: the law of entropy, or the principle that any system tends to change from a state of order to disorder. Or, as my father used to say: "Things are getting worse all the time."

If things are indeed getting worse all the time, if any initial gains we make in an activity will decline and disappear, then the corporate and academic sectors' insistence on constant improvement is more than simply misguided. It is a lie, a malicious lie told by those who are on a sinking ship and who want to distract the crew with petty competition while they themselves sneak off on a lifeboat.

This is why I want to propose something, not only to my fellow Eddan members, but to every faculty member at the University of X: stop trying to justify yourselves. Stop writing teaching philosophies that claim that you've discovered some novel pedagogical technique, when in fact what you did do was teach the same material. Stop pretending that you are the same brilliant iconoclast you were when you were twenty-five, if now you are forty-five. Stop giving into the fallacy that you must obey the fascist logic that permits no stasis, no stability, no normalcy.

How mid can you go?

That lecture was easier to write, record, and upload, and it contained no scandalizing material about Syd.

So it took around two weeks before its effects became apparent to me. It was first picked up on some blog for higher education; the writer singled me out as a representative of what she called the "slow education" movement (like the trendy "slow cooking" fad, I suppose). And that brief and modest internet attention was quietly pleasant, I must admit. For a few hours, as I sat at my kitchen table and sipped my coffee and watched as students walked from their dorms toward their classes, I began to fancy myself as having started a project of true merit. I enjoyed a luxury I hadn't permitted myself for some time: browsing the online news, watching knitting videos for sweaters I would never knit, even catching up on some celebrity gossip, although I recognized few of the names and faces. It was all empty and sweet.

After a few hours of that hazy reprieve, I received a mass email addressed to all faculty. It was a press release for a new publication in *Science*, the world's premiere general interest scientific peer-reviewed journal. It was a big deal to be published in *Science*, both due to the journal's prestige as well as the fact that major media outlets circulated the findings of certain *Science* articles. And so that email asked me to join the Provost in congratulating Syd Niall for leading a research project that indicated that certain organisms exhibited capitalist behavior if allowed sufficient conditions to reproduce and evolve. That was what the hackneyed email said, at any rate; perhaps the Provost's public relations department wanted to avoid details that might have undercut the thrill. We all had to wait a few more days until that same PR rep sent us all a link to a video showing Anderson Cooper, the famous CNN correspondent, interviewing Syd. I sat as if turned to stone as I watched Syd and Anderson smile, wondering dully where my recent moment of well-being had fled. Syd wore glasses for the interview. His hair seemed more yellow and less brown. He smiled tensely and puffed out his cheeks a few times in nervous exhalations, but that only made him more charming, and he otherwise came across as calm, modest, even self-effacing. Cooper was an intelligent interlocutor, and he and his team knew how to formulate questions that demonstrated passing knowledge of Syd's work, and he summarized that work into language that non-specialists could understand.

"Dr. Niall, you used ants as the subject of your experiment, but your results have ramifications for humans."

"Yes, Anderson, we used ants because of several well-documented traits that are found in human cultures as well. Ants keep slaves, for instance. Within a colony, there is a division of labor. Colonies go to war with one another. We wanted to test a hypothesis for another similarity: that, if left alone and if apportioned appropriate and sufficient resources, our ants would adopt an organizational structure similar to Capitalism."

"Wow, that is an impressive goal. So what did you find?"

"We set up three cases: a control of 21 colonies, subject to a 'normal' or typical set of adversities (we studied a species of ant native to Western Australia, so ants there deal with alternating dry and monsoon seasons, as well as alternating food scarcity and abundance, which leads to competition for food; and predators); a group of 21 colonies beset by greater-than-typical challenges, and finally, a set of 21 colonies at categorically optimal conditions. They had enough, but not too much, food and water, ample space, perfect weather, an absence of predators, and all the time in the world.

"What we found happened late in the experiment period, so about 30 queen lifespans in, or a little over three years. Ant society is already quite regimented and hierarchical. But here, a colony began to divide itself into workers who no longer worked, and the rest (the queen and her attendants, regular workers, the nurses). The mutinous workers began to attack systematically the means of production (the place in the colony where food is 'digested'), but, instead of killing their adversaries, they barricaded them within their workplace, wherever it was. If those workers balked, a renegade would come in and attack. Eventually it became clear that these renegades had expropriated the expropriators. If you march around the colony waving the queen's head in your mouth it's relatively easy to maintain control of the survivors."

"You're serious?"

"Quite. We were as surprised as anyone."

"Wow. So, your conclusion . . . ?"

"Our conclusion is that, in the very specific case of this type of ant, a capitalist type of social structure eventually replaced what we previously thought was a more or less static social structure."

"Okay, so what are the ramifications for humans?"

"Well, we can't go overboard in claiming some truth for humans, given that we were working with ants. I think that the truly interesting finding in all of this is that we've decoupled, for the first time ever, Capitalism from human beings."

"Exactly—I can't conceive of Capitalism among dogs or fish."

"Nor can I. To be clear, this may be the extent of the affinity: with ants exclusively. But even if it ends with the ants, it shows that Capitalism is a behavior, or, rather, an evolutionary step appropriate when certain conditions are met. It could be likened to the transition from gills to lungs, or from hooves to digits."

"Dr. Niall, does this imply that humans were destined to become capitalists?"

"I wouldn't say that."

"Okay, let me ask a different question. Does this imply any sort of inevitable consequence to there being enough food and water and resources for a species to develop?"

"I'd need a lot more data to answer that, Anderson."

"Fair enough, for another time then. Fascinating work, it's been a pleasure . . . "

. . . and that was all, at least for the interview. It was also the last time that the public was to hear Syd speak for himself. Two days after the CNN interview first aired, Breitbart ran a story in its ongoing series, "Idiocy in the University," on the University of X's "brilliant, earthquake-predicting professor who is alleged to have severely beaten a female colleague, is having an affair with another female colleague, and received taxpayer support to research the claim that ants are capitalist." I had never before read anything from Breitbart, so I didn't know at the time that the article's innuendo and sarcasm were simply how Breitbart treated non-conservatives. Anyone who listened to his interview or read the *Science* article could tell that, in his own way, Syd had just done for the field of evolutionary biology what Darwin had done for the field of biology: create the possibility for an entirely new field. Aside from Leta, no one came to Syd's defense. The Eddans, under the apparently new leadership of Philip, publicly declared their disagreement with the premise of Syd's ant research and asserted that there was nothing in Capitalism to make it an inevitable evolutionary step, for humans or any other species. The University of X, meanwhile, placed Syd on paid leave for the remainder of the academic year. And the next discussions from CNN's webpage referred to Syd as a "troubled" and "disgraced" faculty member who, in his private turmoil, embodied both the best and worst aspects of American academia.

Leta, meanwhile, used subtle and explicit means to show her support for Syd. While she never acknowledged the Breitbart slight, she did repost his past and current work, including his ant article, on her own website. She held his hand whenever they appeared together on campus. And she kept mentioning his name in Eddan correspondence, which, oddly enough, I still received.

I had intended on uploading yet one more Eddans speech, which I had written fairly quickly. It went as follows:

There are two paths today, just like the two paths in Parmenides's poem. One path is TRUTH, and, if we follow it, we will not err. The other path is OPINION, and is comprised of truisms that have never been questioned. Following this path will lead us to doubt, conjecture, and misunderstanding. The trouble is, we can't discern between these two paths. We don't know which of the two is the path of TRUTH. And so we hesitate between the two, and that hesitation will cost us dearly.

One of the paths is the pragmatic one, because it is backed by empirical data. It would have us believe the three laws of thermodynamics: 1) the law of conservation of energy, meaning that there can be no perpetual motion machines; 2) the sum of entropies of interacting thermodynamic systems increases; and 3) the entropy of a system approaches a constant as temperature approaches zero. To summarize these in lay terms: "You can't win, you can't break even, and you can't even get out of the game." These laws and this path hammer into us a sobering message: that we cannot create something out of nothing, and that we will need to work ever harder in the future, harder than we are currently working, simply to maintain what we currently have. These thermodynamic laws and this dark outlook are rooted in our observations of the world and universe, and they assume that there is no primary mover, no ultimate cause, just a hardly understood Big Bang, some initial explosion that set all of this chaos, including us, into being.

The other path would have us believe in the miracle of spontaneous generation, that something can be created from nothing, that businesses can and should expand constantly.

In other words, that M = C = M, Marx's famous equation: in plain language, it says that money can be exchanged for commodities, which are then exchanged for money of a different (hopefully greater) value. And if you are listening to me attentively, you are probably thinking that I have already tipped my hand, and am depicting the first, pragmatic path, the scientific one, let's call it, as the Way of Truth. Similarly, you may be thinking that I have written off the second path, the Way of Capitalism, let's call it, as the Way of Opinion.

Only, both paths are the Way of Opinion. Both paths espouse the same belief (and if you don't believe me, just hang on, and I'll prove it). And both paths derive power from this narrative of antagonism that pits one against the other. For, what spurs the need for constant growth in Capitalism? Marx shows us that it is the declining rate of profit that assures that capitalists must never remain still. Capitalists must grow in order to stave off decay. Expansion wards off contraction.

My goal in speaking to you today is to propose that the Way of Truth is no way at all, but rather an immanence. We are already floating in this truth, even bathing in it. And thus it is so difficult to discern, this Truth, because it leads us nowhere we want to go.

The Truth is this: we are in a cycle of expansion and contraction, growth and loss, life and death. We may kid ourselves into believing that there is some final arrival, a final score, a last chapter, against which all is measured. Only, nothing is final. Capitalism's great lie is to convince us that there is an ending, but the path I am indicating to you all entails merely seeing the circle we are all repeating. The cycle is the Truth, not some happy ending, nor some disaster.

I include that speech here as an example of the self-indulgent pseudo-philosophy I had wanted to write. For, in my heart, I had already lost my convictions in

Marxism, realizing that I had perhaps never believed in Marx as a policy maker, but rather as a diagnostician. Marx excelled at identifying the problems of the Industrial Revolution, but he could not solve them. Just as I could search for a diagnosis for my own illnesses without ever curing them. The night before I planned to record that speech, I recall a few thoughts before falling to sleep: the word that Bartleby, Augustine, and Constantine all used in their conversations with me: mercy. If there is a circle, it is because something regenerates that which is broken, dead, or diseased. Mercy, not truth or power or righteousness, but mercy. My last moment of consciousness before sleep was that of a thought that rang out almost audibly, spoken by a female voice: "That Truth, Annika, is that God loves you and all of us more than we could ever understand."

CHAPTER TWELVE
Mercy

THE DEAN CALLED TO TELL ME THE NEXT steps. We were now ready to enter the next phase, and the Eddans would be charged with its administration. All humanities departments were to be phased out, or "sunsetted" as he called it, within five years. Effective immediately, admissions to undergraduate and graduate humanities programs would cease. Current students would be allowed to finish their degree within five years, but no longer than that. The Eddans would have a generous budget of $100,000 for the next five years to stage collaborative events demonstrating "synergy" and "cross-disciplinarity." At the end of those five years, I would recommend two to three faculty members to continue work as researchers at the University of X. The other members of the humanities faculty would receive notices of non-reappointment. The Dean stated in no uncertain terms that I was, and would remain, the leader of the Eddans.

I hung up the phone, and, for the first time in my life, I prayed.

Or rather, I tried to pray. Prayer is like ultraviolet lights that are momentarily lit in a room that is normally pitch black. Before the lights were turned on for the first time, my eyes had grown accustomed to the darkness. I had learned to discern certain shapes, such as a table at the other end of the room, or a dresser against the wall facing me. Over many years of fumbling and groping, I had arrived at something resembling an understanding with this darkness. I knew more or less how not to walk into things, although I stubbed my toe occasionally. I congratulated myself for not walking head-first into bookshelves. I crowned myself a saint of veniality, for any missteps I did commit were, naturally, the fault of the darkness or my being born without night vision.

During this first attempt at sincere prayer, not a formula or nursery rhythm but an acceptance of Your invitation to have a conversation, You did not illuminate this darkened room. Rather, You revealed (with a sort of black light) creatures painted in neon pastels as dubious as caricatures of Elvis on black velvet. These creatures varied in size and appearance. The most harrowing were small and insect-like, sporting fluorescent yellow-and-pink stripes and dots. These, prayer has since taught me, were the sins of whose existence I was more or less already aware: anger at Syd, sloth, envy of Leta. These sins were relatively small because I had already acknowledged them as sins that I needed to redress. I was a recidivist sinner, but at least saw myself as a sinner rather than a holy person.

Yet the more I prayed, the more You revealed fluorescent creatures in that dark room, creatures that had previously been invisible to me. Walls that, I could have sworn, had been bare and dark were now effectively teeming with unknown vermin. Each good session of prayer revealed more sins, most of which were trifles on their own, but, in combination, threatened me with discouragement. The little room of my soul began to receive more ultraviolet light that, in turn, adumbrated creatures of sin, the awareness of which I had previously lacked. With the light of prayer, I could now make out a red dragon of anger that I fed and nursed with venom not only toward Syd but everyone I believed had wronged me. And while I knew that the anger in this room was some sort of beast, I could not apprehend the size or shape of the beast, nor could I tell what the beast was doing there, only that it breathed slowly. That much I could tell, for the decorative patterns rose and fell in time with a soft rumbling bellow.

The room of my soul was illumined, and I saw not only the red dragon of anger, but a yellow-striped beast lying partially on the floor. It is more precise to say that the beast was a colossus, and that it took up what space it could on the floor, and the rest of its body folded at a ninety-degree angle to line the wall and ceiling. When I first saw this animal, I flinched in horror, knowing that this particular sin must have been gargantuan, that it was everywhere in me and had been there since my childhood, only I had been too blind to see it. I had walked on top of the beast, and had even mistaken its mass for stability and truth. You later told me, Lord Jesus, that this was the sin of pride, and that it was my gravest sin. Pride made me turn away from God and make myself a god. It led me to look for a worldly paradise. It goaded me to seek the future in tarot and Marxist theory and even my blood work. It hardened my heart so that I looked for fault everywhere except myself. It inculcated an anxiety for worldly things, for the world itself; for even when I saw the impermanence of the physical, I reneged on that knowledge by maintaining my attachment to the physical.

I have never stopped praying since that day. In a sense, I could stop my memoir here, for the only thing that matters is that God granted me the grace to listen and talk to Him. The rest is unimportant. Still, I should summarize what happened to the Eddans.

Two days later, Leta reached out to say that she had thought long and hard about it, and decided that she was ready to follow my suggestion for an event at Pelican Cove. I could not believe that she bore me no ill will. But we met in person, and I could sense no insincerity about her. She was forlorn, but somehow chose not to turn that sadness into anger. She made no mention of Syd. And so the plans gradually came together, between that first conversation and subsequent discussions with the Eddans. We agreed to meet on the last Saturday of the month, to coincide with the new moon. Thirty-eight people, all affiliates of the Eddans, committed to showing up at eight in the morning, a veritable miracle considering that most academics have difficulty functioning that early. Then again, Leta promised to distribute marijuana-laced muffins, and said that a friend would bring psychotropic mushrooms, so there were incentives to participate. Leta coordinated details for her side of the event: there would be music broadcast over loudspeakers, and she asked certain members of the group to wear simple costumes that she had sewed together. "Simple" turned out to be an understatement, for the costumes consisted of tubes of fabric for the head and arms. The cloth was a light green polyester, the sort of thing one might see in the 1970s film, *Logan's Run*.

I was not surprised, indeed, I had expected, to hear in Leta's music the same little motif that by then had followed me from Hippo back to Los Angeles. Leta had responded well to my invitation to prepare music over which I would deliver a speech. After we set up Leta's generator and her two little speakers onto large granite slabs that loomed over the tide (that was fortunately low and several feet away), I sat on another slab that was uncomfortably pivoted at a twenty-degree angle from the horizontal, just enough to make sitting painful. I spread out three sheets of paper with my text, securing each sheet from the wind with a pebble. I cannot recall what I said. The text surely must have had to do with financial cycles and natural cycles, and the need to opt out of Capitalism, although I fear that I didn't get very far. Leta's music lulled me. When I moved my head even slightly, white squiggles like firecracker contrails shot out from the center to the periphery of my field of vision. I had experienced such "visual disturbances" before, but they had been occasional and never lasted longer than a few seconds. Now, though, they resurged every time I inhaled or pivoted my head. A small black dot, outlined with white, appeared at the center of my vision, and persisted whether my eyes were opened or closed. The black center was fixed, but the white outline flickered like the corona of a solar eclipse.

I slumped forward and my mouth began to drip drool onto the rocks. Leta called out to me and I asked her for an aspirin, and she began digging for one in her purse. She yelled for others to look for aspirin as well. Someone asked if weed would help, and Leta snapped back in response. The black spot began to grow in diameter, with my vision slowly being subsumed into it. As the spot grew, sound disappeared, or rather hollowed out, until the lapping waves vanished, leaving only Leta's motif looping thin as if through two empty tin cans connected by a string. The most striking aspect of the ensuing minutes was their utter absence of worry. I suppose that I understood enough to know that I was experiencing a transient ischemic attack (TIA) or mini-stroke, and that the next seconds would determine whether I came to, as if after fainting, or else sustained damage to my brain or lungs or other organs, due to a blood clot. If I knew enough to call out for aspirin, then I knew the danger. And yet, as the black dot overcame all else in my sight, I felt as I did so long ago when I was a toddler, riding around in my mother's Volkswagen Rabbit as she ran errands. Everything we saw and did and heard was just so, just stops along the way, a way that could not be questioned any more than could the wind or gravity. And in place of the anxiety I might normally have felt, I saw that all of the anxiety throughout my life, for my health and supposedly impending death, were all stratagems my little ego employed in order to clamor for its own importance. In wallowing in my unnamed sickness, wasn't I just insisting on my spurious right to good health? And in focusing on my hastening demise, wasn't I implying that I deserved immortality? And the thought continued even as the black dot dispersed briefly enough for me to look on the cove cliffs from below (for I was being carried by two or three people back up from the beach) that all my anxieties, for the country and the university and the future of humanity, were themselves passive means of asserting *my* territory, *my* preferences, *my* identity, onto a world that owed me nothing.

And yet, while I could claim nothing for myself, certainly nothing due to merit, could I not admit that I, as undeserving as I was, had been showered with graces and blessings, favored with aptitudes and talents that gained me access to schools, universities, and eventually my job, however conflicted about it I was? And never mind the practical details: could I not admit that I had been given, GIVEN, not only the ability to write about ancient history, but a clear love of the past, of the Roman Empire in whose fall I so desperately wanted to see a mirror for my own circumstances?

In short, was it not true that my chronic unhappiness was the result of ignoring all that I had been given, and instead insisting on my primary role in a series of events over which I had no control?

There was no cove. No one was carrying me back up the cliffs. My body was undetectable. There was no black spot. There was only a void, and then Bam was sitting next to me as if he had always been there. He was wearing a white and red polka-dotted dress shirt and paratrooper pants that had been cut off below the knee. He sat with his left leg crossed so that his meaty calf was resting on the right knee, and his fingers were playing cat's cradle with some string. As he was contorting strange configurations in his hand-loom, he said, "Dear Annika, divine mercy is a golden thread that weaves its way into everything. You need only look for it to find it." And he put down the string, which I then saw for the golden thread it truly was, and Bam let fall away his human form, and I recognized him as the dragon I had seen in my dream after first meeting Syd, and then re-encountered when I sent myself away to commandeer Syd. Bam was the dragon, but now he revealed himself to me completely. His wings opened wide and high and shaded me from nearly all of the sky, if it was sky in the background, for I could not tell if we were outdoors or in a hospital or somewhere in the ether. He was a red dragon, and yet he was not reptilian. There was nothing hostile to him. He had been there, the whole time, from my earliest memories onward, and he had never left me. He watched over me as only a *malayka* could do, and even let me see him, for most *malayka*s never permit themselves to be seen. He breathed, "Christ loves you as His own, and His Mother does too," and then he was no longer there.

Much later, Leta was sitting beside me and leaning in so that her arm gently cradled me. We were in a hospital emergency room, and when I said that I needed to pee, she walked me over to a common restroom shared by five patients in separate rooms. I was lucky; the bathroom was vacant. "The IV will make you have to go often," she said quietly. Her voice was careful and kind. Her face was drawn from lack of sleep. She turned her back while I urinated, and when I finished, she walked me back to my bed. It was as if I had been asleep for two years and was now weakly awake. I tried to interpolate for the time I had been out.

"I'm so sorry this happened," I began.

"Don't be silly," Leta said as she grasped my hand. "They say that you are stable, but they need to keep you for observation a little bit."

"How long was I out?"

"Not sure. It couldn't have been longer than a half-hour. That's how long it took for you to be checked in."

"Oh." There was a white board affixed to the wall on my right, and in green block letters, someone had written: "Watch for symptoms of hyperviscosity: dropping, aphasia, loss of consciousness." I understood the letters and the words they formed, and the significance of those words: that the doctors and nurses were watching for symptoms of a blood clot in the brain. I knew that I should be afraid, but all I felt was sorrow for derailing Leta's event. The absence of fear was itself almost alarming. Here it was, this fate I so dreaded, close enough to have touched me, and yet I was not even remotely fearful.

Leta stayed in that chair all afternoon. A doctor visited at some point a few hours after I had been checked in to report that I'd be cleared for discharge pending a CT scan of my brain. I thanked Leta, and told her that she should go home, "to Syd," as I put it. She looked down and smiled, and despite my worry-free haze, I braced myself for the reproach I knew I had coming. Still, she said nothing, and her smile was neither forced nor pained. She said goodbye not long after, pressing my hand and making me promise to call her tomorrow. And all I could feel during the remainder of that hospital stay, through the CT scan that showed my brain to be uninjured from the episode, was that light pressure from Leta's hand to mine, a warmth that said more than anything I had ever learned about mercy. For I would have refused to believe Leta if she had said that she forgave me for destroying Syd. But I could not refuse to believe the gesture of taking my hand, or the mercy that made her gesture possible.

Given the structure of this memoir, the natural next step would be to include my last YouTube speech, the speech I wrote the day I returned from the hospital, and recorded the following day. But I am tired of reading my speeches, and my interpretations of others' speeches. Besides, it can be summarized concisely. I renounced all my accusations against Syd. I said that I was disgruntled at Syd spurning my advances, and avenged myself by claiming that he had beaten me. All of my injuries were self-inflicted, I stated. The video lasted less than a minute, and I shut off my computer immediately after uploading it. I never again checked my personal account, never again went on YouTube, and so I don't know what the reactions were in the comments section. I walked on the blue-and-beige carpet of the basement of the library one last time and exited the building like I left the campus, as if it were just one more day of dissipated effort. I emailed a brief letter of resignation to the Dean, providing neither reasons nor justification. I stayed in my apartment with no break for the ensuing week, finalizing travel arrangements and tying up loose ends of grading and bowing out of publication commitments. And then I was gone, from the University of X as well as Los Angeles, with only two bags, one for clothing and one for a laptop and a few books, on a plane to Reykjavik. A day and a half later, I was sitting in a lounge in the commuter section of the Reykjavik international airport, waiting for the commuter plane to Bíldudalur. Depending on the season, there were either one or two flights a week, weather permitting.

The plane was late, already by an hour, when I finally noticed the man sitting alone, off to one side. His black hair was in a loose ponytail. I didn't need to see his face to confirm what I already knew, that it was Bam. He was his normal self, no wings or tail.

"May I sit down?" I asked.

"Of course," he said with a big grin. "The thing I love most about Iceland is the wool." And indeed, Bam had a long sleeve of something in white wool. He was attempting to knit with five double-pointed needles, but it looked a mess. "Did you know that you can buy wool in gas stations here?"

"No, I didn't."

"It's true! I've seen every gas station in Iceland, and every single one sells wool. Often of good quality! All local."

"Winters here are long."

"And folks need some way of passing the time," he nodded solemnly. And then he fixed his concentration on his knitting. I didn't know what to say, so we sat in silence. His wool was in bad shape. Yarn is supposed to be arranged in balls or skeins, but this stuff looked as if it had been dumped haphazardly. I looked closely, and Bam's fingers detangled the yarn just before he then set it up for a stitch. What came out on the other end wasn't elegant, for the yarn was the scratchy kind for which Icelandic sheep were renowned, among knitting enthusiasts, at any rate. It was fuzzy, but it did gel into a recognizable object, a half-finished sleeve.

I tapped my fingers on the table, and without looking up, Bam said, "I'm sure you can appreciate the metaphor."

"I don't follow."

"Taking something messy and making something good with it."

"Oh, is that what this is? Your knitting, that is."

He smiled ruefully. "A bit. I do like knitting. I liked it before you were born."

"I see."

He sighed with what I thought was contentment, and asked, "So you've sent yourself away again?"

"This isn't sending myself away. It's . . . ," I trailed off.

"It's real?"

"I suppose. More real, at any rate."

"I don't think you believe that for one moment."

I frowned. "It's no way to live, sending myself away. I never learned a lot of things because I could leave whenever I pleased. I'm a prepubescent old maid."

"Moving up here certainly isn't going to broaden your horizons, though."

"Who's to say? And, anyway," my voice dropped as I grew serious, "why are you here?"

Bam's smile evaporated as he too became grave. He put down his knitting. "We aren't done."

"What does that mean?"

"Just that: we have more to do."

"Who's 'we'? I didn't realize 'we' were doing anything." My voice grated petulantly.

"Did you think that your work was finished the moment you issued your apology? The moment you walked away from your job? Come now, you need to think more carefully than that."

I said nothing, and looked through the terminal windows. There were no planes at any of the gates.

Bam took up his knitting. "The plane isn't coming."

"The flight hasn't been canceled. The lady at the counter told me that the plane would be here by 10:30 a.m."

"That was an hour ago."

I got up and asked at the counter. The attendant was baffled, for she had just received word that the pilot phoned in sick.

I walked slowly back to the table where Bam was sitting. My feet were tingling, the way they do when the blood starts flowing after a foot or leg has fallen asleep. "Now what?" I asked, utterly deflated. "I don't have a place to stay in Reykjavik. I don't want to stay in Reykjavik . . ."

"We aren't going to stay anywhere. We are going to Bíldudalur."

"What, are we renting a car?"

"No."

And though I thought of a dozen indignant retorts to Bam's proclamation—that it was lunacy, too far, that I was in poor health, that I didn't want to be with him or anyone else—I followed him meekly, almost as if I had had another attack and was now incapable of resisting. We exited the airport and Bam hailed a taxi, and within an hour we were in central Reykjavik with its throngs of tourists and neatly dressed twenty-somethings. Bam held the car door for me to get out, but, from there on, he walked ahead, his bearing making it clear that he would countenance no argument. We walked west to the large performing arts center, but instead of entering we took a service road that encircled the building. Once arrived on the other end of the center, opposite the city, it was a short descent to the docks, where the water was exceptionally dark, an inky oily black unless the sun, already setting, hit it at just the right angle. The liquid was cold and brackish. I wondered at my sense of repulsion, for I had always been a partisan of the sea, no matter how cold or turbulent. Bam looked at me, for the first time since we arrived in Reykjavik, and said, "You are not seeing the sea, but rather the promises of the world." And dumb as I was, like some drowned kitten, I said nothing to challenge him or even ask for clarification.

We were now walking on a quay that jutted out, without berths or perpendicular traverse sections. At the end of the wharf was anchored a single-mast sailboat, probably thirty feet long. I know nothing about boats and so know nothing about how to describe that particular boat. It was painted white. There was a little cabin with four portholes. There were two dinghies attached to right and left walls. Bam was untying the rope that fastened the boat to the dock. I sat down on the closest available object, a storage locker next to the ship's wheel. Bam fiddled with some of the equipment, and the motor began to turn, and then we pulled away from the dock, making a slow turn toward a breakwater that shielded the harbor from the open ocean.

I couldn't make sense of the water, which shone an appropriate slate gray near the horizon, but was still sludgy jet around the boat. I must have looked stricken, for Bam said even as he was steering, "Your anguish is a sign that you understand the gravity of the situation. So, even as you suffer, take heart that it is not for nothing." He said this lightly, with a smile. The sun was now near the horizon, but there were no sky colors that would have suggested a sunset, no yellow or orange, just gray to the west, and an expanding black to the east. I was now lying rather than sitting on the locker, and Bam came to help me to my feet. We staggered over to the ladder, climbed down to a tiny room with a single bed, and Bam tucked me in and closed the door after himself. I slept for a long time, until the sky was again light with the earnest but enervated northern sun.

Everything was different when I awakened. The boat was now no longer white, but dark wood. There was no longer any motor noise. There was no motor, but the mast now had three sails, rather than one. There was rigging scattered all over the place, on the mast as well as attaching the sails to the deck. Bam was no longer manning the helm. There was a heavy cold wind like I had never before felt, and the boat was rocking with waves between fifteen and twenty feet. Within seconds, my face was stinging with cold, and I ran to the closest railing to vomit. Those waves called to me as I retched into them. They told me in their slick glossy black language that the time had come: "There is no point in pretending otherwise. The decline has happened, the limit has been reached, we have surpassed the tipping point. Jump in, and accede to the inevitable." With one hand I clung to the railing, and I tried to wipe my mouth with the other, but the wind kept blowing spray into my eyes and mouth. Bam, meanwhile, was climbing the mast to the crow's nest. I shouted, "Come down! Don't leave me alone down here!" But my voice could not carry over the water and wind, and Bam kept climbing, eventually disappearing into the basket that looked so far and small from the deck below. I clung to the railing, the boat rocked back and forth, and the storm blew on, when Bam reemerged from the perch and *deployed his wings*, wings that I hadn't noticed on him. He looked straight ahead toward the bow, and his wings were glorious, of feathers that were metallic and iridescent.

I cannot go further in writing, yet I must. I know that any reader must conclude that I am lying or mad, or just lost in my stupid tales of sending myself away. And yet, with all the humility I can muster, I can only repeat that it is true, all of it. Bam steered the ship through the storm, somehow, despite standing in the crow's nest and not touching the wheel. I restrained myself from jumping into the ocean, which continued to speak of decline and entropy. The boat inched northward along the west coast of Iceland, and eventually the weather calmed; I could see from the vertical cliffs that we were rounding the Westfjords. We turned toward the right, and descended into the fjord in which Bíldudalur was nestled. The sun eventually dried out the deck and me with it, while Bam's wings shone blindingly, and I dozed. My mouth tasted like salt and oil, and I wondered if I might ever stop hurting, just as Bam climbed down the mast and gathered rope that had been strewn on the deck. He folded his wings, and then they were gone as if they had never been there; but there was a slight figure waiting on the little dock to which Bam steered the boat. We pulled to shore, and Bam tied us to the mooring. I knew before the ship was close enough to recognize him that the figure was Augustine.

Bam called out and there were then others who lifted me up from the deck. They had a stretcher and carried me off the boat up a short distance from the water to the little red house where I had sent myself away so many times. The others left, and Bam waited outside the front door, to be "on lookout," as he put it. Augustine sat quietly at the kitchen table. I must have slept, for I don't remember how I got from the stretcher to the kitchen, and how long it took; it might have been days. Eventually, I was well enough to walk and talk. I voiced my surprise about that to Augustine, who shrugged and said, "All things are possible with God."

We sat and talked for hours, until well past nightfall. It is difficult for me to remember specifics from our conversation. Suffice to say that he had come here to Bíldudalur, to "make things right," for Bam had told him that I was in a bad way. It was good that I had confessed, he said, but now I was in the gravest danger, for the evil one is never more aggressive than when he senses that he is about to lose a soul. "He will tell you all sorts of half-truths in the hope that you will lose your resolve. What have you been thinking during your voyage here, Annika?"

"That the laws that govern the world also determine economics, politics, my health, even my love. Everything must decline, friction will grind down everything. I will soon die because the mutant alleles in my blood are crowding out the healthy ones. Capitalism will overtake everything and destroy the planet." I was now crying, and Augustine said, "Now that's enough, my child, no need to carry on so. Shh . . . " And it was like that for some time, the older man comforting the younger-but-still-old virgin who sobbed like a lost child.

"The evil one told you mostly truths. In all ways but one, he is right. The world will eventually grind down to dust, and nothing will survive. What was it that you told me you like to say to your students? 'The physical world will let you down' — that's it, isn't it? We are stray plants clinging to a vertical rock face," — he gestured to the cliffs high above the fjord—"and there is no chance that we will survive. There is no chance to create a financial system that is self-sustaining, that will not demand exploitation, because profit is always declining"—and I didn't ask how he could have known Marx. Augustine continued, "You have heard in the music of your friend the melody, the motive, I think you called it (and I again reeled to hear him speak in such modern terms) that starts high and descends, and then returns. It is not by accident that you have heard this, Annika." And he went on to talk of grace, the gift of God's love that humans have never deserved, but that He gives us freely, all the time and forever, not because of who we are, but because of who He is. His eyes filled with tears as he spoke like a kindly madman of seeing the face of Jesus, of a love that we knew before we knew anything, a warmth and embrace that preceded any decline. Grace and its direct manifestation, mercy, were here before the physical world with its deprivations. And they are quiet and mild—he held his wrinkled hands up to his ears to listen—"You must try very hard to make them out, for the world is so loud in comparison." Grace and mercy may be quiet and invisible, most of the time, but they are everywhere—"I challenge you to find a place where they are not," he said, admonishing me with a wagging finger. "Mercy is the motive that always returns; it is the exception that gives the lie to all the laws of your science, because it always grows. The Resurrection repudiates the tyranny of death, of decline, of decay, of vanishing profits and crumbling institutions and broken hearts, of time left and inevitable progression. The empires of my day and your own, whose falls so enthralled you—they are as nothing compared to this love, this grace and mercy."

He spoke for much longer than I can write here. I am putting down only the moments I can recall. There was so much more; he told me of the beauty of Paradise, of

Our Lady, who exudes at once the greatest joy and the deepest sorrow. He spoke of his own tears of happiness at seeing his mother Monica and son Adeodatus. Most of all, he talked of seeing Our Lord's face, and of the love that he had simultaneously known since before birth, yet that met him as unknown and inconceivable. The light in the fjord was now gone; there were a handful of lights on the shore opposite Bíldudalur, perhaps from a cabin or even some boat anchored for the night. It became increasingly dark in our little red house as well, and I felt no need to get up to turn on a light. This ended up being fitting, for Augustine eventually stopped talking and bowed his head, and I sat in silence, and then he was no longer there. I stared at his empty place, and I must have closed my eyes, and then the faint gray morning sky awakened me later. Bam was nowhere to be found. I have never seen him since. I will spend whatever days are left to me in this little house, awaiting that love of which Augustine spoke. It has not shown itself often to me. But it is better to wait for something good than for a decline or catastrophe. That is what Augustine told me.

www.ingramcontent.com/pod-product-compliance
Lightning Source LLC
Chambersburg PA
CBHW032145020726
47496CB00003B/730